The Hunger Scream

Ivy Ruckman

WALKER AND COMPANY
NEW YORK

   First published in the United States of America
in 1983 by the Walker Publishing Company, Inc.

Library of Congress Cataloging in Publication Data

Ruckman, Ivy.
   The hunger scream.

   Summary: A girl who suffers from anorexia struggles to
deal with the problem.
   [1. Anorexia nervosa—Fiction] I. Title.
PZ7.R844Hu 1983   [Fic]   83-6522
ISBN: 0-8027-6514-9
Printed in the United States of America
10 9 8 7 6

For Ruth
who has the staying power of her name

One

Lily stood well back from her bedroom window, shivering, her hands rubbing her upper arms. She couldn't take her eyes off the Perrys' circle drive.

"You're late, Daniel," she whispered. "Seven minutes late!"

The sheers billowed inward, filigreed with early morning light. They brushed across her bare legs and clung to her bikini under-pants. Quickly she stepped back, ignoring the sensation on her skin.

Daniel wouldn't recognize her after being away a year. She was a different person altogether. Warming herself against the chill, she stroked the sides of her new, lean body and laughed softly to herself.

Where are you, Daniel Perry? You're slipping.

Then Lily heard the thud of the Perrys' front door and her heart began to pound. She stepped behind the drapery, though she knew perfectly well he couldn't see her there at the second-story window at 6:07 A.M.

She heard the sounds of gravel crunching underfoot. He was walking down the drive. There. Into the lighted asphalt circle now. Four footfalls...the theme of "Rhapsody in Blue"...and he was off running, his body moving without resistance.

[1]

He was wearing jogging shorts and the same gray sweat shirt he'd ruined last summer carrying the hundred-pound drum of chlorine for her dad. That was typical of her parents, to think of Daniel when muscle was needed Now that Daniel and she were older, the fact that he was black caused sudden, sometimes frantic maneuvering on their part. They were scared to death she'd fall in love with him.

Daniel was out of sight now, down the hill approaching the Walker-Nelsons', and Lily realized she had ten minutes to dress if their paths were to intersect the way she'd planned. Lily hoped he was still the same—her Daniel, dearest childhood friend. Was he making a statement wearing that old gray sweat shirt? *I haven't changed—see?* Well, she had. Lily Jamison had changed a whole lot. For the first time in her life, her body was more important than the clothes she put on it. She hadn't learned it from her mother, who prized fashion above all else, or from her father, who cheerfully doled out the dollars for their swollen wardrobes. Her teacher had been Daniel himself, and he didn't even know it.

Lily hurried across the deep carpet, the color of ripe cantaloupe, into her spacious bath and dressing room. She touched the light panel with her elbow, then blinked rapidly into the wraparound mirror confronting her. It offered three identically slender, fair-skinned Jamison girls in place of one—a schizoid experience so early in the morning. Lily smiled as she ran her hands across her flat stomach and down to cup the hipbones which were beginning to show. She was getting there.

Onto the scale before dressing, she confirmed her weight at nearly a pound less than last Saturday, marked it on a chart she kept behind her closet door, then got into her warm-ups and jogging shoes.

At the last minute, which was very unlike her, she exchanged the T-shirt that read "Joggers Do It Running"—one her mother

[2]

had never seen—for a long-sleeved pullover that screamed "Thin Is In" in tall, skinny letters of lime on navy. The decision had something to do with Daniel, but there was no time to analyze it.

Listening for sounds as she passed her little sister's room, Lily slid her hand along the balcony rail, then negotiated the winding stairway and the broad foyer in a matter of seconds. Outside, she kept to the grass, avoiding the asphalt drive until she was well out of earshot. Nothing annoyed her mother so much as the sound of nylon runners smacking the cul-de-sac surface on Saturday mornings, the day "everyone" slept in.

At the bottom of the hill where Oak Grove met Danish Road, Lily turned left under the archway of trees. Daniel would have gone right, running past the abandoned church and the old sugar mill.

Are you still logging five miles, Daniel? Or is it ten this year? Please... today be predictable!

Tempted to cut herself short, Lily nonetheless kept to her plan, threatening grave self-denial if she'd miscalculated. Her Nikes chopped off the distance in fractions of seconds. *Crunch, scrunch, crunch. Scrunch, crunch, scrunch.* Eventually another jogger approached from the Pinebrook development. The woman waved as she passed. Lily smiled, trying not to break the level of concentration she had to maintain.

At the entrance to Pinebrook she made her turn, then picked up her pace a little. The breathing was easier, she was getting her second wind. It was her legs that sometimes failed her. Why did she feel so much weaker now than she had in the spring? She'd never been so disciplined, but her stamina was off. Nearing the end, she began to recite the little jingles that kept her going.

Finally, Lily could see the stone pillars of Oak Grove once more and the sign that read "Private Property—No Trespassing." She gulped in the air and began to slow down. At the stream grates she trotted in place, loosening her arms, then her shoulders. She glanced uphill, past the Walker-Nelsons' to the two homes that shared honors at the end of her street. No Daniel in sight. She smiled, expelled the air from her lungs, filled up again. He'd find her here, cooling down. It would look innocent as anything.

One foot braced on the grate buttress, bending forward, stretching...she heard him approaching. She knew without looking that it was Daniel and not the jogging housewife.

Eight, nine, ten, she persisted.

He slowed, but she wouldn't allow herself to look around. *Eleven, twelve.* She changed legs, bending deeply in between.

"Lily!"

She turned.

He stood where he'd stopped, several yards away, breathing hard, hands on hips, a great grin on his face.

Lily's voice stuck in her throat. Though sunrise was officially twenty minutes away, she saw at once that Daniel was different. Bigger, broader. And his voice was deeper. Suddenly she felt as if she'd fallen into a trap of her own making

"Hey!" He walked toward her.

Her insides collapsed.

"I didn't recognize you... "

She smiled back, though she wanted to cry for some dumb reason.

"You know, you're the last person I'd expect to see out jogging. Lily the gymnast!"

"I'm following your example, that's all," she said.

Daniel shook his head and laughed. "Looks like you dropped some pounds since I was home."

"Twenty-eight."

"You look terrific." He circled behind her, rubbing his chin. "A little skinny. maybe."

"Oh, *you!*" She stuck out her tongue, then hated herself immediately. That's what her sister Juju would do.

They started up the hill together, walking slowly, self-consciously.

"When did you get home?" She knew, of course.

"Last night."

"Your mom said you'd be going to the university now. Didn't you like Stanford?"

Daniel shrugged. He looked up at the overhanging trees. "I belong here." His gesture meant *here*, Oak Grove Drive. It also meant *here*, Canyon City, Colorado. She wished it meant *here, walking beside you*, but she knew it didn't.

"Besides, I missed my family," he went on.

"Did you really?" Lily stared at him. Incredible! She couldn't wait to leave home and do her own thing.

"I even missed you," he said.

Lily felt herself blushing.

"I did. How come you quit writing?"

"You never wrote back."

"Oh...was that one of the conditions?"

Lily bent down and pulled up a fistful of long-stemmed grass, roots and all, but Daniel anticipated her. He jumped aside, shielding his face.

"Don't beat me, Massa!"

Lily took off, chucking the grass clump in a lateral pass. He caught it, chucked it back. Laughing, she ran ahead of him to the footpath, where she waited for him to catch up. He had changed. Last year he would have chased her.

He arrived panting, pretending to exert himself.

"Fake!" she accused.

"Phony!" he shot back.

"Falseness personified!" they declaimed together, cracking up. It was an old routine, harking back to the time they'd had

[5]

parts in a school skit when she was a sophomore and he was a senior.

"So I'm the sophomore and Lily Jamison's the big senior this year?" Daniel said, snatching the thought right out of her head.

"I was bigger as a sophomore, if you remember."

"Aw, quit fishing. You know you were cute."

"One hundred twenty-nine pounds on a five-seven frame doesn't spell c-u-t-e."

"That depends on bone structure, muscle tone, lots of things."

Can't you see? She wanted to say. *I look so much better without all that baby fat.*

Now he was looking uphill toward his house. He wouldn't go straight home, would he? Didn't he want to be with her?

"Daniel...we could have coffee in the gazebo...before anyone's up."

He hesitated.

"Come on." She nodded in the direction of the footpath. "You haven't forgotten the shortcut, have you?"

He trotted behind her through the trees to the creek, then alongside it for a hundred yards to the rear approach to the Jamisons'.

"Hold on," Daniel said. "Why don't I go home and shower? I'm kinda sweaty. And how about me bringing some toast?"

"Terrific! Twenty minutes?"

"Gotcha."

Laughing, they smacked hands and parted on the run, Daniel returning to the footpath that followed Willow Creek behind the Perrys' property, defining the boundaries of the two cul-de-sac homes by its gentle meanderings.

She hasn't changed at all, Daniel thought. *Still as intense as ever, only now she's a bone. Why can't Lily do something halfway...like everyone else?* Daniel popped two extra English muffins in the toaster. He'd have to fatten her up.

[6]

His mom had written about the Jamisons. "Lily's a scarecrow," she'd said. It hadn't made sense until he saw her. On Mrs. Jamison, who was thin bordering on fragile, the high-fashion look seemed right. "It defines her," his mother had said once, meaning: She's a fashion illustrator. Why shouldn't she look like one? The models she drew were eleven heads tall and emaciated, terrific Geritol candidates. Reclining, their hipbones stuck up through their expensive underwear like shark fins. Lily had shown him into her mother's studio one afternoon. Recognizing a Karen Jamison illustration was a cinch after that.

Daniel buttered the muffins, then spread each with generous amounts of whipped honey. He stacked them in a basket, then slipped through the kitchen doorway and down the back walkway. The house was still quiet as he left, though Skipper and Trinh had begun whispering in their room upstairs.

Sure enough, Lily was in the gazebo waiting for him. He could see her through the screened windows, pouring coffee from a ceramic pot into matching mugs. The sun was up now, giving Daniel a long, exaggerated shadow which preceded him up the stairs.

His first impression was a pleasant one. The gazebo was dappled with light and filled with the good smell of coffee. Then he focused on Lily.

"Welcome home," she said, her eyes bright.

"I'm much obliged." Daniel bowed slightly. He didn't want her to see his face, which must have registered distaste. In shorts and a sleeveless blouse, Lily looked very thin indeed.

Two

"Lily, you're not going to start that business with Daniel all over again?" It was Karen Jamison, launching Saturday morning with an accusation.

It was nine-thirty and all four Jamisons were seated in the breakfast nook.

"What do you mean?" Lily's father asked, looking up from the paper and the real-estate ads he was memorizing. "She hasn't even seen Daniel."

"Oh, yes, she has!" Juju piped up, grinning under a grape juice moustache. "I saw him, too, an' he hugged me."

Lily's daggered look cut out Juju's tongue. "Tell Daddy about it," she invited sarcastically, though sarcasm didn't always register with her little sister.

"Will somebody tell me what's going on?" Whatever-was-going-on was interesting enough to make Lily's father put the classified news aside.

"Daniel and Lily and me already had one breakfast out in the gazebo."

"June Jamison, were you invited?" Mrs. Jamison asked, taking a half slice of whole wheat toast on her plate.

Juju stuck out her chin. "Yes. Daniel hisself invited me."

"*Him*self," corrected their mother.

Lily's father was looking at Lily, still waiting for an explanation that was rapidly becoming a redundancy.

"I saw Daniel when I was out jogging. I asked if he'd like some coffee, that's all." Lily looked pointedly as her mother. *If anybody's starting anything, you are, Mother dear!*

"I think we should discuss this in private," Mrs. Jamison said, returning the pointed look across the table. "Private" meant she'd do all the discussing, without Juju's big ears or her husband's interference.

"You're making too much of it." Lily's father helped himself from a dish. "Try the eggs, Lily, while they're hot."

"I'm not hungry, thank you." She passed them on to Juju, who never turned down anything.

"Of course you're not, if this is breakfast number two," her mother said. "Did you eat anything solid?"

"She took one bite of Daniel's muffins." Juju, child reporter, chronicled the news again. "They had honey on top. Daniel ate four an' I ate two." She giggled again.

Lily wondered how she'd get through another year with such a brat for a sister. Little Junie—surprise or mistake, Lily wasn't sure—got by with everything. Lily had to be the Big Example. First...oldest... *Pin all your hopes on me, why not?* Why couldn't *she* do as she pleased for once, not as *they* pleased? Why was Juju excused, catered to like some household god?

"She's only three," their mother had said for a whole year. That was when Baby June declared herself, poking a stubby finger at her chest, "Me Juju." Then she was "only four," which meant open season on all Lily's things—her cosmetics, her school papers, her charcoal sketches. Now she was "only five." *Hey, when do I get an 'only'? I'm only seventeen. Has anyone noticed I'm overdue? When do I get to have my way?*

"You'll be here this afternoon, won't you, Lily?" her mother asked, breaking into her litany of hate.

"I'm always here."

"I want you to watch June while I make a delivery to Dorbach's."

Lily nodded as her mother continued to plan her day for her.

"Why don't you invite Erica over to swim? You two haven't had a falling out, have you?"

"Mother, we ride the school bus together every day."

Her mom looked at her coolly over her cup of black coffee. "Well, I was beginning to wonder. She practically lived here during the summer."

"Better get your swims in," her father rejoined the conversation. "Have to close the pool before long."

"Can I invite Daniel to swim?" Juju begged, bouncing up and down on her chair. "Can I?"

Good idea, Lily thought, sectioning her grapefruit.

"Juju, what's this with Daniel? Little Skipper's your age." Karen Jamison touched the corners of her mouth with a pink linen napkin. "You may ask Skipper to swim if Lily stays with you."

They're such hypocrites, Lily thought, offering swims to their black neighbors, inviting them to barbecues, exchanging liberal talk and enlightened views. *But keep your son away from my daughter!*

"Where are you going today?" Lily looked at her father. He was wearing his tennis whites, handsome as ever with his blond hair and moustache and his Robert Redford good looks. She knew what the clothes meant, but she'd better make sure. With both of them gone, she would invite Daniel. She'd call Erica, too. Her being there would make it okay.

Howard Jamison pushed his chair back from the table. "I'm

playing tennis. Want to meet me for a late lunch at the club, Lil? You could drive over and bring Juju."

She managed a smile, but shook her head no.

He stopped behind her chair, squeezed her shoulder. "Never get to play with my old tennis partner, do I? Say, when are you going to start eating again? Your mother and I worry about you."

"Howard," Mrs. Jamison interrupted, "the doctor said not to nag."

"Reminding isn't nagging, Karen. Besides, doctors don't know everything. Will you make yourself a good sandwich?" He tilted Lily's face so she had to look up at him.

"Yes, Daddy."

"Ham and cheese and avocado and pickles..." He showed her how thick it should be.

Lily licked her lips, though the image was turning her stomach.

"And I'll have a tomato malt!" Juju announced, her mouth full.

Their dad laughed as he bent to kiss Juju on top of her curls. Lily looked away. She couldn't remember the last time her father had kissed her.

"Lily, stay a minute," her mother said a little later. "I want to talk with you."

Lily knew she should have excused herself from the table when Juju did. Now she was trapped.

"I'm not concerned about Daniel's being here for coffee," her mother began in this sincere voice Lily had come to suspect, "but it worries me that you never have room for anyone else so long as Daniel's around." She rearranged the creamer and sugar. "He's home now for the entire year. Remember, Lily, he's been away on his own...well, you know...he's a college man now. You're still in high school, in many ways an inexperienced little girl."

And you never let me forget it! Lily looked down at the napkin she twisted under the table.

"We all know how you feel about Daniel. It's no secret. Howard knows. Daniel's parents know. And certainly *I* can see why you're so fond of him."

Can you?

"But the thing for you to concentrate on now is accomplishing something. You have your whole life ahead of you. Schoolwork, your activities, friends, your family. You've been accepted at the university and at Radcliffe both." She paused. Her voice took on an edge. "Are you listening to me, Lily?"

"Of course I'm listening."

"Do you understand what I'm saying? It isn't because he's black or that we're prejudiced."

Lily couldn't control the smirk that took possession of her mouth.

Her mother straightened, setting her coffee cup firmly against the saucer. "Who sold the Perrys that house next door? Your father did. In an effort to stop red-lining in this community, he sold that property to a black family. Does that smack of racism to you?"

It smacks of good business, Lily thought, recalling her father's version of the transaction—that had been told and retold.

"Oh, Lily—" Mrs. Jamison pushed her chair back. "I'm really out of patience with you. Can't you see we're thinking of you? Your father and I love you very much. We want what's best for you."

Lily sat there, trying to believe it. She squinted at her plate in an effort to remember how things used to be. Her mother had had lights in her eyes once. Back in the days when she did Lily's hair in curls every afternoon and dressed her up for dinner, back when Lily had been the baby doll.

"Mother," Lily said in a soft voice, trying hard not to sound belligerant, wanting just this once to make her mother understand, "Mother, Daniel and I are best friends. We grew up together. We like to do the same things, sometimes we even steal each other's thoughts. We're not going to..." How could she put it? Her mother was already shaking her head, waiting to break in. Lily sat forward, talking over her. "We're not stupid!"

"I know you're not. I also know you've been taught to be moral. We expect you to behave yourself, under whatever circumstances. It's just that, well... friendship can lead to something closer. At your age, Lily, sex just isn't important. With the right person at the right time..." She ran her hands nervously along the tablecloth. "Sex is for later on."

She'd said it! Her mother finally said the word *sex*. Lily thought of Jeanne and Wendy, junior varsity cheerleaders who wore their honor society pins upside down at school the day after they lost their virginity. She thought of Erica's indiscretions, which were too numerous to mention. She herself didn't *want* a sex experience. Couldn't her mother see that? It was the guys, the ones who'd taken her on dates, who were all after something. Daniel was the only one she could trust. He'd never, ever tried anything with her.

"What I'm saying," her mother said, clearing her throat, "is please don't make a spectacle of yourself by pursuing Daniel Perry. It's vulgar and unladylike at your age. I don't think his parents like the idea any better than we do."

Karen Jamison was on her feet, stacking the dishes and gathering the napkins. It was over. They'd had their little "talk." Lily was now expected to conform.

Lily excused herself, cheeks flaming, feeling more soiled than the egg plates from breakfast.

She went upstairs to her room. The air there was heavy with depression. She opened a window, sat down beside it, staring at nothing. Hopelessness crowded in on her.

"Meet Lily Jamison, nonentity," she said ruefully. "Her mother chooses her clothes, dictates her hair style"—her glance took in the creamy white of her bedspread and the bright pink of the accent pillows—"even decorates Lily's room to suit herself. Now she's selected two colleges for her daughter and alerted her own sorority at each." Lily sighed.

Her father was almost as bad, dragging her through ten years of tennis lessons when she'd rather be playing with her friends. For some reason, though, she felt he valued her more than her mother did. In Karen Jamison's eyes, she was still a child, stupid and inept. *You bet, Mom! Tell me how to behave in great detail so I won't slip up and be an embarrassment!*

Lily picked up the patchwork pillow on the window seat and held it against her cheek.

"It doesn't go with the contemporary decor of your room," her mother had said a year ago. "Why don't we keep it in the studio?"

But Lily loved it and wouldn't give it up. Grandma Perry had made it for her from Lily's old flowered sundresses and Daniel's cast-off denims. It was her pillow, as much treasured as any of her stuffed animals had been. No way was her mother going to hide it in storage!

Abruptly, Lily's face contorted. The room blurred. With sudden vindictiveness, she hurled the pillow across the room, setting a Boston fern spinning in its macrame hanger. Biting her lip until it bled, she still couldn't hold back the tears.

Three

Daniel didn't go straight home after leaving the gazebo. There was a place on the stream he had to see first. He'd thought about it a lot out in California, especially the week he'd turned down four fraternities and the honky president of one had referred to him as a "snotty black, the worst kind." At Stanford, he'd just close his eyes and zap himself back to the hideout. Instant relief!

Today the path beckoned him as always, drawing him into the shade of the larger trees below his house. He thought of the picture in his high school lit book that stood opposite Robert Frost's poem. Daniel's path, too, was "the one less traveled by"—or it had been, back then. It wasn't a secret place anymore, of course, especially since Skipper and Trinh had come along. Even his mom went there to read sometimes, to get away from the phone and Grandma.

Now, seeing the hideout again, Daniel laughed aloud.

Two immense boulders, deposited by some Ice Age glacier, stood like fortress walls imbedded in the streambank. They were overlaid by a slab of granite. The summer he was nine, Daniel had spent a whole week excavating rocks and debris until the hollow place inside was big enough to hold three kids his size.

Daniel scraped up a pile of leaves for the floor of the dugout before crawling in on his hands and knees.

It's smaller! He looked to both sides and overhead. No, he was bigger, of course.

He listened. The stream, reduced to a trickle by the dry September, was the only sound. The sunlight through the willow leaves made shifting patterns on his tan cords. He tossed a twig in the water, watched it turn, then disappear from sight. He felt totally safe here.

He'd come home from Stanford looking for a safe place. He had to admit it to himself, even if he couldn't say it to anyone else. He had bombed out. C's and D's were failing grades. In his mind, at least. And when he was notified that the track scholarship wouldn't be renewed, he gave up trying in the classroom.

He couldn't compete with the sharp, privilege-bright guys and their superegos. They could screw anything, including the academic system, and make it look good. He was out of his league at Stanford. His high-school GPA, a 3.74 that made his dad beam and sealed his grandma's pride forever, didnt help him understand the theory of quantum mechanics. What good was being the Clarkson Humanities Scholar if you couldn't pass the math requirements for beginning computer science?

Even living in the dorm with a slick operator like Morris Kuchen hadn't improved his chances of making it. He sharply remembered Valentine's Day and unwrapping the macrame owl Trinh had knotted for him. Daniel had hung the strange bird — one eye slightly askew — above his bed, and it made him laugh just to look at it. But when Morris went into convulsions, inviting the whole floor in to see it, well, that was different.

"How much do you charge for decorating services, Perry? Maybe you can find something equally tacky for my side of the room." Morris could be a very superior son-of-a-bitch when he pulled out all the stops.

Daniel ran his hands over the pebbly rock surfaces on either side of him. He was glad to be home, glad to have another crack at school, but he didn't have illusions this time. What he had were doubts—lots of them.

Then Daniel thought of Lily and of all the times they'd hidden out here together. Lily had envied him his hideout. It was the one thing he had that she didn't. Trouble was, she wanted it totally integrated. He remembered how she'd taped a sign overhanging the granite slab: "Wayfaring strangers! Free lodging. Come Ye on in." He'd torn it down, replacing it with "Hard hat area. Enter at your own risk, stupid!"

A year ago, he and Lily had said their good-byes in the hideout. Sitting comfortably squished, he'd held her hand. Well... she had held *his* and he hadn't minded.

"You'll forget me," she'd said.

"Huh-uh!"

"I know you will. It happens to people all the time."

"We're not *people*," he'd said.

"What are we?"

"We're... you know... best friends."

He wasn't any more eloquent now than he'd been last September. How was he going to ask Lily what was wrong with her? Daniel bit the side of his hand as it rested on his drawn-up knees. Was she sick? He thought of leukemia. What was that other one? Anemia? *Pernicious* anemia. He'd have to ask his mother about Lily. Something was wrong.

Then he heard his name being called.

"Daniel, we're eating!"

"Coming!" he hollered back.

Skipper met Daniel at the door of the screened-in back porch, grabbed him around the legs, and hung on so tight Daniel couldn't move.

Skipper squealed as his big brother lifted and held him overhead.

"Now what do you say, huh?" Daniel swung him down and

under one arm, carrying him inside like an animated football—arms, legs, mouth all going at once.

"Touchdown!" Skipper yelled.

Daniel set him down and paddled him on the rear.

Nine-year-old Trinh was pouring orange juice at the table as they came in. She looked up at Daniel, her dark eyes shy, pleased. She ducked her head when he winked. Half Vietnamese, half black American, his adopted sister was already the beauty of the family.

Their mother had her back to them at the stove. Daniel stepped noiselessly across the room and hugged her from behind. "What smells so good?"

"Apple pancakes and bacon. Your favorite breakfast."

"*You* don't get any of it," his dad said as he entered the kitchen.

"Morning, Dad." Daniel grinned. "Are you man enough to stand between me and my breakfast?"

"I doubt it, not anymore. You been out running already?"

"Yeah, had to check out Danish Road." Daniel crumpled a strip of pilfered bacon in his mouth. He felt sheepish, letting his eagerness show. "Who's building next to the Sugar Mill, anyway?"

"Tanner. He tore up that nice stand of wood along the creekbed. Condominiums, I hear."

Daniel noticed the gray in his father's curly hair. It hadn't seemed so pronounced last night at the airport.

Florence Perry motioned them toward the table, a platter of breakfast in one hand, the coffee pot in the other. "Homecoming lesson number one, Daniel. Nothing stays the same."

They took their seats then, Daniel pleased to see his old place at the table waiting for him between his dad and Trinh. That was the same at least.

"This little peanut sure has grown." Daniel patted his sister on the head. "You speakee English now?"

"You tell Daniel," Mrs. Perry urged Trinh. "Remember what you were going to say? Next time Daniel said, 'You speakee English,' you were going to say—"

"*Non!*" She lifted her chin.

"*Non!*" Daniel repeated. "What's that mean?"

"*Je parle le français seulement.*"

Daniel let his face register astonishment. "Well, blow me over!"

Trinh giggled.

"I can say French, too." Skipper waved his fork in front of Daniel. "*Un, deux, trois.*"

"Son-of-a-gun!" Daniel exclaimed, rolling his eyes. "Culture's so thick around here, I may have to go back to the raunchy old dorm."

"Pass Danny the bacon, Paul," his mom said, keeping an eye on her son's plate. "I saved some in the warmer for Grandma, so there's no shortage."

"Where is she?" Daniel asked, feeling suddenly guilty that he hadn't missed her this morning. So it wasn't his place at the table anymore. It was Grandma Perry's. No one had bothered to add an extra chair yet.

"She was worn out from last night." Florence Perry glanced at her husband. "Besides, I thought it would be nice to have breakfast alone…just the five of us."

Daniel understood and was grateful. It was hard on his mom, having Grandma the past two years. An hour after his dad left for the university each day, his mom took off for her job at Family Services. Dealing with other people's problems didn't make handling her own any easier. "Grandma had a bad day and I've just put her to bed," she'd write in a letter, or, "I found Grandma feeding grass to the Walker-Nelsons' horses. She thought she was home in Memphis."

Once while he was gone, Grandma had walked all the way to

the sugar mill by herself. "Cain't stand bein' cooped up in that house!" she'd told the man who picked her up and drove her home again. She hadn't been out of her head *that* time.

Yes, Daniel knew perfectly well why Grandma was allowed to sleep in some mornings. Breakfast without Grandma was his mother's equivalent of Daniel's retreat. Such a little space he and his mom needed—one breakfast, one sun-dappled hideout. He smiled at her across the table. "I'll help you with Grandma now that I'm home."

She smiled back.

Four

Lily scooped up one tablespoon of cottage cheese from the carton. Carefully she centered it on the slice of tomato nestled on a lettuce leaf.

"To be tempting, a salad requires color contrast," her mother-the-gleeful-gourmet was always saying.

Lily rummaged through the jars in the fridge, extracted a black olive from one, halved it for the top of her salad, and stood back to regard her creation. Lily, too, was acutely color-conscious when it came to food. Lately, since her diet, the colors in a meal gave her more pleasure than the eating, which always carried its own price tag. The way she figured it, a thousand calories a day meant maintenance; anything less meant losing weight, ridding herself of the ugly rolls of fat over her knees and belly. The excess was disappearing. Two more pounds to lose and she'd be perfect. She calculated the cost of the salad: twenty-five calories plus six for the olive half.

Lily picked up her plate. She'd eat outside, on the deck. Slowly, quietly. The salad would have to last until dinner.

Suddenly, out of nowhere, there was Juju, blocking her exit by the sliding glass door. "Daddy said you had to make sandwiches. It's for your own good!"

Tight-lipped, Lily turned back into the kitchen, pulled the peanut butter out of the cupboard, extracted a loaf of bread from the bread box, and slammingly tended to Juju's demands.

Everything was for her own good! Even Juju was starting to sound like *them.*

"You mad at me?" Juju's voice was small. "I didn't really want a tomato malt. I was just kiddin'."

"I wouldn't make it if you did."

"I like chocolate better." Juju pulled herself up on a stool at the eating bar.

Lily didn't measure anything, merely dumped it in the blender —ice cream, malt, the end of a can of Hershey's. The gross sweetness of it made her mouth turn down, though a fist of hunger tightened in her stomach as the mixture whirred and bubbled.

"Yuk!" she muttered as she poured the malt and stuck a straw in it.

Juju rattled on, oblivious. "Skipper said he ate spider soup once. His grandma makes it all the time."

Lily smiled in spite of herself. Impulsively, she bent down and kissed Juju on the cheek. "You'd believe anything, you old gooney bird."

"I would not!"

"Would too! Now eat your lunch before everyone gets here to swim. I want you to help skim leaves."

Outside, Lily gratefully dropped into a lounge chair.

"His grandma also makes rattlesnake stew." Juju was talking to herself in there. She didn't care if no one listened. It had never been that way with Lily. She *cared* that no one listened. They'd ask her opinion, then disregard it, yakking on and on as if she hadn't spoken a word. She'd been quiet at Juju's age, a model child, they said. Too bad. Now they expected her to remain mute and obedient forever.

Lily wondered, her eyes narrowing, what they'd do if they

knew her real, true thoughts. Sometimes she felt like giving them a hint, something subtle, thrown into the conversation when they were preoccupied—which was always.

"How was school today, dear?"

"I ran a pen up my nose."

"Marvelous! Keep up the good work." Said while smiling. Or maybe, "I think I'm going crazy, Mom."

"It's not something we do in front of the neighbors, dear."

Lily recognized the guilt fingering her insides. When had she stopped loving her mother? She used to worship her! As a little girl, she'd been able to call up her mother's dear face whenever she needed comforting—in school, at a friend's house, during tennis lessons. There were times away from home when she literally got sick because she missed her so much. What had happened between them? How had they lost out?

Daniel was the one she really cared about now... maybe because he cared about her. He was the one who thought she was funny, who called her from Stanford on Groundhog Day, who noticed when she didn't write. He always considered her opinions worth listening to.

"How'd you make out in that all-male chemistry class?" he'd asked her in the gazebo that morning.

"The hardest part was washing test tubes," she had confessed.

"You've got it made, Lily, being smart, white, and rich. Besides being a woman, of course."

"You're half right. I'm a white female."

They'd laughed and he had held up his cup for more coffee.

"What I hear is that you've got it made, being smart and black," Lily countered, "besides being a Stanford man."

He'd given her a peculiar look then, which she couldn't quite read.

"I need all the help I can get," he'd mumbled.

"No, not you, Daniel. You're really... super!"

"Yeah? Well, you just think so because I put up with you all these years."

He had looked right into her eyes when he said it, but when he stopped smiling, she caught a glimpse of the sensitive Daniel inside the hard-muscled exterior. She was sure he'd been about to confide in her.

Then Juju had shown up in her pajamas and bare feet and Daniel had her on his lap, letting her snuggle into his chest. After that, everything they said was interrupted or had to be explained. Finally, they made Juju run back to the house for a glass of milk and slippers, but by then the magic was gone.

Now Lily nibbled at the olive that topped her salad. At least Daniel was coming back over to swim, she had that to look forward to. But it couldn't be just the two of them. Erica was coming, too, her string bikini stretched tight over her jiggling flesh. A sketch of Erica, her mother had once said, could be accomplished with a series of overlapping ovals. Lily couldn't understand what guys found so sexy about her. To think she herself had looked like that a year ago. The convex stomach, thighs that touched, pendulous breasts—everything moving in a symphony of flab—ugh!

Lily ate the cottage cheese in dainty bites. She'd stretch the meal as far as she could. If she was hungry after her swim, she'd halve a fresh peach. One half a peach, twenty-five calories. She set her plate aside and lay back on the lounge, feeling the delicious warmth of the sunlight as it penetrated her skin.

Lily sighted along her slim legs, bent them slightly, wondering how she could appear to best advantage when Daniel arrived. Her shinbone made a sharp line on her lower leg. She sat up to run her hands over the ridges, smiling to think of all she'd managed to accomplish toward body control. If only her strength kept pace with her determination. Fatigue was the enemy. Maybe she should try the high-protein powders.

"None of those in this house!" her mother carped whenever Lily brought up the possibility. "Those diets are dangerous." Lily sank back into the lounge and closed her eyes against the sunlight. *Well, so is eating, Mother dear!*

Daniel heard Erica before he saw her. The sound of her clogs preceded her up the hill. He dropped down on the grass at the Jamisons' curb and waited. If she was as much of an eyeful as he remembered, it'd be worth the wait. As soon as she saw him, both arms flew in the air.

"Danny!" she called. Her white robe blew open and flapped in the breeze.

Daniel waved back and started downhill to meet her. Erica was the most spontaneous, irreverent person he'd ever known. Pure spunk! She was wild as a jackrabbit.

"How you doin', Babes?" He grinned broadly as they met.

She grabbed his arm and pulled him close. She pushed the mane of dark hair out of her eyes with her free hand and laughed up at him. Same old Erica, clinging, laughing deep in her throat. She gave him the bold look that had been her specialty since she was thirteen and discovered sex. At that time she'd scared him to death. Now she was just being Erica. Daniel laughed right back at her.

"Is it really you?" she said, setting him free with a little shove.

"Sho' nuff is! Anybody miss me around here?"

"Of course! We all missed you."

"Old Pillow Ticking know I was gone?"

"Hasn't anybody told you about her?"

Daniel shook his head. Pillow Ticking was a mare that virtually became Daniel's when show time rolled around each year. Though not a show horse herself, she was bred for the fine stock she produced. When Erica's family took the horses on the road, they hired Daniel to look after the stock left behind.

[25]

"P.T. didn't foal this spring."

"She didn't?"

"My dad said she was pining for you." Erica's laugh rippled across the Jamisons' driveway. *She's always so pleased with herself*, Daniel thought, wondering if breeding made a difference in people, too.

About then Juju came bounding through the gateway that led to the backyard. "Is Skipper comin'?" she asked, making a beeline for Daniel. He swung her around enough times to make her squeal, then set her down.

"Yeah, he's *comin'*. But you better go help him. He can't find his swimming suit."

Juju put her hands on her hips like one disgusted five-year-old waiting on another. "Men!" she muttered and marched off toward the Perrys'.

Daniel and Erica exchanged looks and burst out laughing.

Lily was waiting at poolside, her eyes closed behind a pair of huge sunglasses. Daniel winced to see her in a bikini, but Erica, apparently used to the new ascetic Lily, joyously bubbled on, making a big thing of Juju's "men."

"My sister," Lily lowered her shades, "will do or say anything to get attention."

"Unlike you, huh?" Erica mumbled as she slipped out of her robe.

Daniel whistled between his teeth at the sight of Erica, his brain screaming, "Centerfold! What a fox!" Immediately he was sorry. Lily was his hostess. Quickly, Daniel moved to recover from his fumble. "How will I keep this silly grin off my face around you two bathing beauties?"

It worked. Lily stopped scowling. "Grins we can handle, right, Erica?"

"You said it!" And Erica hit the water with a flat racing dive.

Daniel stood there, waiting politely to see if Lily wanted to swim now or talk. She patted a chair next to the lounge and he sat down, kicking off his thongs, letting his towel slip to the deck. The air was late September cool, but the sunlight felt good. He stretched out his legs and sighed. He was home, with friends. This year would be better.

"I'm glad you called me," he said.

"Well, enjoy. Daddy's closing the pool October first."

"Now, why's he doing that?"

"It's the fault of the OPEC nations," Lily said and giggled. She leaned back again and closed her eyes.

Erica's kick turn, coming at regular intervals, sounded like a dolphin turned loose in the Jamison pool.

Later, after they'd each done laps and played Marco Polo with the little kids, they stretched out on the redwood sun deck and compared tans. Daniel won. He wasn't as light as his dad nor as black as his mom, but he was a nice rich brown—like Grandma Perry, who claimed some English duke had come skulking around among her ancestors. Being the authority on color, Daniel helped the girls classify theirs. Erica, they decided, was Mediterranean Bronze. Lily was Nordic Sunglow.

"What color am I?" Juju insisted on playing.

"You're blue," Lily snapped. "Now wrap up in your towel or I'll make you go in."

Skipper was too busy getting at his popsicle to enter the color contest. He sat there next to Juju, legs spread, dripping and shivering as he tugged at the wrapper with both hands.

Daniel, amused, nodded toward Skipper. "Ever see such concentration? Here..." He ripped the paper off and handed the popsicle back.

After they'd soaked up all the afternoon sunlight that was available and sent the little kids off to play, Lily brought out a tray of vegetables, dip, and drinks.

[27]

"The Tab's for me," she said, allowing Erica and Daniel to choose their own.

"You need Tab like I need that sociology test tomorrow," Erica said as she opened a fruit drink.

"You're not still on a diet?" Daniel asked. "I bet you don't weigh a hundred pounds now."

"I do!" she protested. "I was a hundred one this morning."

"Lily, now that's the max!" Erica pulled herself up onto her elbows to face Daniel. "I keep telling her she's too skinny. Don't you think she is? She won't listen to me."

The iced Tab was raising goose bumps along Lily's arm so that the look she gave Erica was cold and shivery at the same time.

"Well, it's true!" Erica stood her ground.

"You don't want to make yourself sick," Daniel said.

"I'm in better shape now than I've ever been. I don't see *you* out jogging, Erica."

"Oh, Lord, no!" Erica laughed. "I ride, remember?" Then, under her breath, "...sometimes."

Daniel handed Lily the tray of vegetables. "Here, have some. I don't want you to starve to death."

"No, thanks."

"Go on," he persisted. "You've got to be hungry after swimming."

"She's never hungry," Erica said, regarding the onion dip on her carrot. "How many calories is this? How would it hurt you, one little ol' dollop of sour cream?"

Lily shuddered and stood to look for a wrap. Daniel was glad. Her shivering had increased so visibly, he thought her bones might start to clank. Covered with a giant white bath sheet, she looked 100 percent better.

"See? You need a little fat to stay warm. Look at me." Erica opened her arms. "I'm not even chilly."

"You *are* well insulated," Lily observed.

"You're damn right."

Daniel guffawed.

"So let's change the subject," Lily said. "I like being thin, okay?"

Erica's face softened. "You probably think I'm jealous because I hate diets, but I'm not, honest. I just think someone ought to tell you when to stop. You look...like a stick. Doesn't she?"

Daniel shrugged. "I never saw anything wrong with the old Lily."

Lily leaned toward him, her eyes snapping. "You don't remember what you used to call me? You don't remember telling Skipper to throw the ball to the *wide* receiver? I was always the wide receiver, ha, ha! And how you used to pass me in the hall at school, saying 'Fat Stuff' out of the side of your mouth—"

Daniel threw up his hands. "Guilty! Guilty! But I didn't mean you were fat, like overweight or anything." "Curvy" was what he'd meant but couldn't say.

"Interesting semantics." Lily spat out the *s*'s. She took off her big glasses and looked haughtily past both of them. "Fat doesn't mean *fat*. Tell me about it!"

"Don't be a pain, Jamison. We love you—fat or skinny. Don't we, Daniel?"

"Why, sure."

Lily hid behind her glasses again as her eyes filled uncontrollably.

"Why is everyone so obsessed with my looks? It's my body, my life—or have I missed something?"

"Forget it," Erica said, dipping into the sour cream again. "Let's turn the page, get a new topic. *Daniel*! Tell us about Stanford, why don't you?"

"What's to tell? I squeaked by, that's all."

"We know better, don't we, Lily?"

[29]

Lily stood and pulled her towel close around her. The after noon had suddenly gone flat; she no longer wanted to be with her so-called friends.

As Erica continued to ask Daniel about his freshman year, Lily busily gathered popsicle papers and cans onto the tray and made a trip inside. The second time in the house she changed into her warm-ups. She came back to find Daniel and Erica still talking away, looking as if they hadn't even missed her.

"Well, you have to study for a test, Erica, and I have to make up some new cheers," Lily said in a voice too cheery. "Tryouts are coming up and I'm supposed to be helping with the new sophomore squad. So..." She flashed them a smile. "Party's over, I guess."

Daniel and Erica exchanged looks, then stood and gathered up their things.

"Lily was JV cheerleader captain last year, did you know that?" Erica said as she worked her feet into her clogs.

"No, hey, that's great!" Daniel mussed Lily's hair, the way he would Skipper's, feeling suddenly sorry about the afternoon. "No wonder you stay in shape," he added, trying to make it up.

Lily looked at him gratefully, her eyes swimming. Quickly she turned and headed toward the house, waving only at the last minute to acknowledge their thanks.

It wasn't quite two-forty, but the day was over. It disappeared with Daniel's laughter as he and Erica left the yard. The clanging of the gate was the final sound, the end of something so sad and irretrievable Lily couldn't quite identify it.

Lily stood in the kitchen a long time, her fingers clutching the edge of the Formica countertop, her eyes narrowing with each breath.

"I hate them both!" she said between clenched teeth, wanting to run after them, to scream ugly words at their backs. Why shouldn't they know how much they'd hurt her? Why should *they* go off happy and laughing... and together?

When Lily finally let go of the countertop and walked to the refrigerator, the trembling that started in her hands took over her entire body. Quickly she set out the roast remaining from last night's dinner. The butter dish next, a jar of horseradish sauce, the black olives. On the second shelf she spotted three pieces of blueberry pie left in the tin. Standing in the open door of the fridge, using only her fingers, she scooped up a wedge of pie and began devouring it in huge bites. Her eyes were closed so she couldn't see what she was doing, but inside her head the shrill scream of rage went on and on.

Five

It was easy to avoid Erica at school that next week. Lily's father was dropping her off early for cheerleader practice, and at night she caught the late activity bus. The one time she saw Erica coming across the cafeteria, she'd picked up her tray and left. Simple as that. Of course, Lily got the old fish-eye from the lady at the clean-up counter when she handed over an uneaten meal.

Avoiding Daniel wasn't so easy. If he ran in the morning, she'd run after school. If he was out warming up his car the same time her dad pulled out of the garage, she'd suddenly remember an assignment left upstairs in her room and send Juju to tell her father to wait a minute.

But the logistics weren't the worst part. She didn't *want* to avoid Daniel. She wanted to see him, to talk to him. She'd conditioned herself for six whole months to be able to run with him. Even when he'd called to tell her about his university classes, she'd made Juju say she wasn't home, then she hadn't returned his call.

She wasn't *allowing* herself to associate with Daniel.

If she regained the control she lost after their pool party, when she'd eaten everything in the fridge, then—only then—would she permit herself to see him again. She knew she had to be punished;

she also knew what was right for her, though it took a strong will to carry out her own prescriptions sometimes.

Lily was glad to hear the final bell ring on Friday. She'd spent five days working with the sophomore hopefuls before and after school. Moving woodenly through their cheers or bouncing all over the place, they struck her as being more hopeless than hopeful.

"They're really dismal," Lily said after school, perched on the edge of 'the couch' that dominated Ms. Snell's office. Everyone knew the dance teacher practiced psychiatry without a license all the time, but tonight Lily hoped Snell would skip the analysis. Monday was cheerleader elections and no one was ready.

"Shall we talk about it?" Ms. Snell gave her a syrupy smile.

"We've got to figure out how we'll get through the assembly period," Lily said. "We have twenty-five sophomores trying out, plus the juniors and seniors."

"Oh, Lord!" Snell sat forward, all business now. "That many? None of them dropped out?"

"Not a single one. Two hours of practice a day. And I was rough on them, like you said. They loved it."

"You see why I need you?" Snell was up and attacking the coffee pot. "Cream or sugar?"

"Black, thanks."

Lily studied Snell's profile as she filled the cups, noting with approval how tight her body looked in the leotards, even though the plaid skirt hid her legs—her best feature. Half in, half out of dance costume, always running off to a meeting or clacking down to the office in her Dr. Scholl's sandals, Snell had never been organized in the two years Lily had known her. Tonight was no exception.

Ms. Snell handed Lily a cup of steaming coffee. "Have you thought any more about what I said Monday? Including the sophomores makes my job absolutely staggering. I could kill Bevis!"

Lily shook her head sympathetically as Ms. Snell moved back to her desk. Not only had the district postponed all student body elections until this fall because of school boundary changes, but Principal Bevis was now asking that sophomores—who'd always been song leaders—be included in the JV cheerleading squad.

Lily looked through the steam at Ms. Snell. "I'd like to help you, honest. I just don't see how I can." *I wish she'd quit whining. I'm a cheerleader, not a faculty adviser.*

Ms. Snell took off her glasses and rubbed her eyes. "Okay, I'm going to level with you." She straightened as she said it. "You're the most dependable cheerleader I've ever worked with, but I don't think your health can stand so much activity right now. I wish you wouldn't try out this year."

Lily stared.

"Believe me, it's not just that I want you to train the second-stringers. I do, of course. You'd be my right hand. But you're so underweight right now it's scary."

"I feel fine!"

"You don't look fine."

Lily's jaws worked. She felt color flooding her face. "I don't understand. I just put in a whole week of really hard work with the sophomores. What makes you think I won't hold up?"

Ms. Snell swiveled to face the window, noisily letting out her breath. Lily's mother sighed the same way when she was exasperated. *Snell must really hate me,* Lily thought, staring into the cup at her own reflection.

"How much do you weigh now?" Ms. Snell asked, turning back around.

"I don't know."

"Are you eating?"

"Of course!" Lily felt her eyes flood. First Erica and Daniel, and now *Miz* Snell. Who did they think they were, anyway?

Lily stood and set her unfinished coffee beside the pot. "I have to go or I'll miss the activity bus."

"Don't run off, I'm sorry." Snell's smile flashed on cue. "You know me! Mother Superior, full-time worrier."

"I really have to leave." Lily picked up her poetry volume, suppressing the urge to carom it across the desk into her teacher's face.

"Give me a call Sunday, then, and we'll make up the ballot for the cheerleader election. I'll run it off Monday during the first period. Will you do that?"

"Yeah, okay." Lily laid the list of sophomore candidates—all paired but one—on her adviser's desk. *Let her figure out what to do with the Rogers kid,* she thought as she turned on her heel. *It's not my job.*

All weekend Lily waited for one of the varsity cheerleaders to call her. When she'd tried out as a junior, four different girls had asked to practice with her, and three of them fought over who should get her for a partner. Then there was that night after the football game when Ms. Snell chose her to be junior varsity captain. The squad went crazy. Cory led them in "Give us an L!" They had spelled out her name twice while she stood there with tears running down her cheeks. It was the high point of her life.

By four-thirty Sunday afternoon, Lily knew no one was going to call. She felt hollow, scared. What had happened? Were they jealous? Were they afraid of looking bad paired with her? They could tell she'd stayed in shape during the summer; it was obvious some of them hadn't.

Again Lily checked the clock on her night table. They'd all decided on partners by now. They were at one another's houses—out in backyards or downstairs in rec rooms—coordinating their outfits, practicing leaps and flips. Whether she liked it or not, she had to get on the horn and find someone. If she had to be partners with the twenty-fifth sophomore—a short, fat kid who smelled like he forgot to wipe—it would be a disaster.

Lily carried the upstairs phone into her room and plugged it into the jack. She made herself comfortable on the floor, her back against the bed, and dialed a number she knew by heart. Cory, of all people, should have called her. He was her partner last year, though he and Carol got disgustingly chummy after cheerleader camp.

"Cory," she asked seconds later, "how's it going?"

He said it was going great.

"Who're you trying out with? Snell wants all names in order for the ballot. I can let you be first...." Lily opened the notebook on her knees, then repeated after him in a flat voice, "Carol and Cory." *Sounds like a vaudeville act,* she thought, not quite knowing how to handle the silence on his end of the line. "You guys will be great together."

He thought so, too.

"Want to be first?"

He wanted to be somewhere toward the end.

"Who's trying out *with whom?*" She exaggerated the prepositional phrase. "Save me some time calling everyone, will you?"

He gave her all the senior names. Brian and Susie. Eric and Wendy. All the veteran cheerleaders were paired. Two new seniors and Jeannie were trying out as a threesome. Lily felt sick to her stomach. They'd planned it all behind her back while she was busy with the stupid sophomores!

She laid the phone on the bed, near her ear, and asked him to repeat so she could get all the names down on paper. He obliged.

"I'm sorry you're not trying out this year," came the voice from the earpiece.

Lily grabbed up the phone again. "Who told you that?"

"I don't know. That's what everyone's saying."

"Of course I'm trying out. Why wouldn't I?"

"Carol, or someone...I don't know...told me you'd been sick."

"That's a lie!"

Silence.

Then, "Look, Cory, it's okay. I gotta run. Be on time tomorrow, will you? Snell's having anxiety spasms." She hung up without saying good-bye.

Lily slumped against the bed, her arms around her knees. It was her own fault. Why hadn't she called someone? Why had she waited for someone to choose her? Or maybe it wasn't her fault. Maybe Ms. Snell had spread it around about her being sick so she could use her. Here she'd thought it was so terrific, helping train the sophomores. Well, to hell with Snell! Now she was left without a partner!

Suddenly Lily sat up straight. She'd solo. Brian did last year. Why not? She was better than any of them, at least she was now, having lost the extra weight. Lily picked up the notebook and placed her own name at the end of the list.

"Lily Jamison!" Snell would announce at the mike—with special flair because she was still trying to get on Lily's best side. Then Lily would come out of the wings with a series of back handsprings, ending with a back flip. She'd do the disco routine, the novelty cheer she'd saved for herself. For the traditional yell Snell required, she'd spell out "cougar" or "victory" or something.

Lily jumped up and ran across the room to her closet. She pulled out a red silk blouse with metallic threads. It was perfect. She'd wear her white satin vest and shorts. Most of them would try out in school colors. She'd be different.

Quickly Lily got out of her jeans and into the clothes she'd thrown on the bed. The shorts were too big at the waist, but her mother could fix that in a minute. The vest didn't fit quite right, either, she noticed. No matter, she'd be moving all the time.

Lily posed in the center of her three-way mirror, admiring the sharp angle of her chin and the airy look of lightness about her body. How gross she'd been this time a year ago! Her cheekbones were heightened now. She thought of her art class, how she'd pulled highlights from her first charcoal sketch, kneading the gum eraser, lifting lights in an ecstasy of discovery. Now *she* had the highlights.

Lily appraised herself from all angles. She liked what she saw, but the shorts hung on her. They were way too big. When Lily pulled them out in front, she could see all the way down to her crotch. She giggled at the idea of losing them during tryouts. Definitely they needed altering.

She stripped off again and put on a pair of old leotards for a workout. It would be dark in two hours. She needed every bit of daylight, as well as the entire back lawn, to practice. Suddenly Lily was glad. Grinning and glad. For once, she wouldn't have to worry about someone else's mistakes.

Lily was dismissed from second period fifteen minutes early Monday, along with the horde of sophomores and the handful of upperclassmen who wanted to be cheerleaders. She had butterflies, like everyone else, though the younger girls in the dressing room seemed to think she was beyond all that.

First, Stephanie cornered her. "Scott wants to twirl me overhead in a double stunt and I don't think he should. You know, there at the end?" Her forehead was wrinkled. Obviously she didn't want to be twirled.

Lily zipped up the satin shorts her mom had altered.

"Stick to your routine," she said. "You looked good Friday."

"Oh, great, thanks."

"Lily..." Someone else.

"My partner didn't show." Callaghan looked stricken. "I knew she'd run out on me! Jenny's partner isn't here either..."

"Team up. Let Snell know, then practice a while in the dance studio."

"Oh, God!" Callaghan was still panicky. "We don't match. She's in leotards, I'm in shorts!"

Lily dug in her bag for a key. "My gym locker's 205. Can you remember that? I have leotards in there you can use."

Callaghan hugged her. "You saved my life."

Lily smiled back, fluffing her hair with a vent brush. Had she ever been that rattlebrained?

Outside the dressing room Lily joined the mob backstage, looking for Snell so she could help get everyone in order. Then she spotted Carol and remembered the rumor she started—that someone started—about poor Lily's health. Carol and Cory were talking with Snell. Carol was making big gestures, shaking her head. Something was going on. Suddenly Lily wanted to be in on it.

"That would ruin everything!" Cory's voice carried across other heads as Lily approached them.

"Excuse me," Lily said as she bumped into Stephanie. Then, stopping to talk to Scott, she said, "Hey, you were terrific Friday. Don't try anything new, huh?" Scott nodded as she moved on.

Then Lily heard what Snell was saying. "I can't let her try out alone. Won't you at least ask? She's pathetic, Cory!"

Were they talking about her? Was Snell asking them to *include* her? Quickly, she turned her back.

"I really feel bad about it, but I don't see how you can expect us..." Carol Two-Face was protesting. Lily moved away.

Pathetic! Beverly Snell, who couldn't organize anything, who couldn't even get a husband, thought *she* was pathetic. Lily's eyes filled as she hurried to put distance between them.

"Can you come here a minute?" a sophomore boy tugged at her sleeve.

"No, I can't!" she snapped, heading straight for the tryout order Ms. Snell had posted backstage. Last night on the phone Snell had agreed. "Fine. You can be last." What had happened since then?

Lily checked for her name, though the list blurred in front of her eyes. There it was, at the end. Above hers was the name of Franklin Rogers, the twenty-fifth sophomore. What was the fuss about? Why was Ms. Snell mortifying her?

Lily swung around as she heard her name called. Snell was walking toward her, indicating with five fingers that they had very little time before the assembly bell rang.

"Everybody here?" Lily swallowed, forcing a smile as they met.

"Two absent. I'll ask the students to change their ballots before we start. Lily..." She took Lily's arm and steered her back behind the line which was beginning to form. "I want you to try out with this Rogers person. You'll have time to practice together. We're going to run way over as it is."

"Do you know who he *is*?"

"I haven't the faintest, but what difference does it make? You're all voted on individually."

Lily shook her head. "No way!"

"Now, look, Jamison, I can't have two loners trying out at the end." She was losing her patience. "It puts you both at an unfair disadvantage. Or advantage! I don't know which, but it isn't fair, and I should have told you so last night."

"There he is!" Lily pointed to the fat kid leaning against the back wall. He looked totally out of it, though he had the good sense to be wearing the school colors—green shorts and gold socks.

"Oh, Lord," Snell exclaimed, "is that Franklin Rogers?"

"See what I mean?"

"Why didn't you tell me about him? We could have worked out something...maybe a foursome!"

Lily shrugged. She'd tried to tell her Friday after school.

"Okay, okay." Ms. Snell walked off with her head in her hands, muttering about Bevis and the district and "tryouts which should be held in the spring, for hell's sake!"

Halfway through the assembly period, against the background of chants and cheers and sporadic student participation, Lily began warming up. The Rogers kid watched her but didn't indulge in so much as a deep knee bend. He disgusted her, standing there staring while she limbered up.

"You're a pretty good gymnast," he said after she tried a handspring in the limited space between curtains.

"I need more room," she said, then dipped to touch one toe after another in rapid sequence.

ROWDY, ROW-DY, THAT'S OUR STYLE...
GET UP, FANS, AND CHEER AWHILE!

Carol and Cory were giving it their all. *They sound good. They are good. Lots of smiles and personality.* Lily did a few torso twists.

She frowned, watching the next pair of sophomore girls. They were short on everything—volume, energy, coordination. Their fight yell sounded more like defeat. Even after a week of practice, they'd never quite gotten it together.

It was nearly time for the final assembly bell when Franklin Rogers got his turn on stage. Waiting there beside him, Lily could see how scared he was. Little drops of perspiration stood out on his upper lip. He looked at her sort of wild-eyed as the applause died for the couple ahead of him. "Help!" he said under his breath.

Lily grinned. At least he was game! She admired that. He was a mess to look at, but he was game.

"Go for it!" she said at the last minute.

Franklin grinned back. Then, sticking out his chin, he strode purposefully out to center stage.

Scared now for him as well as for herself, Lily bit her lip and watched with a kind of sick fascination to see what he would do. Everyone laughed, of course. The sight of him was too much. He did a little dance step, something comic, shrugging as if to say, "Aren't you glad it's *my* bod and not yours?" They laughed harder.

Then Lily heard this big, booming voice call out "BOOOOAAAAARD! ALL ABOOOAARD!" The students stopped laughing.

Down on one knee, his right arm the piston, his left working the whistle, Rogers began to hiss and puff. He was doing the steam engine, making such marvelous, authentic sounds that the entire student body was suddenly transfixed.

As the engine picked up steam, the students joined in, chugging faster and faster, louder and louder. Now he was on his feet prancing, his arms pumping, his belly jiggling. Head thrown back, red-faced, the Franklin Choochoo rounded the bend, pulled into the station, slowed, screeched, and hissed to a stop.

Lily couldn't believe the applause. The auditorium was resounding with whistles and cheers. They loved it! They loved *him*. Rogers was a hit! But he wasn't through. He was doing his little steps again, a kind of fat-boy soft-shoe shuffle. When quiet settled over the auditorium, he launched his second cheer in the same incredibly big voice:

"ROLLIN' STOCK, WATCH US ROCK!" (His belly was doing the rolling.)

"STEAM MACHINE, GOLD AND GREEN!" (Now he gave them his profile, handling his excess like a proud stripper.)

"CHATTANOOGA CHOOCHOO, COUGAR'S GONNA *CHEW* ON YOU AND *YOU!*" (Suddenly he was all over the place. The choochoo train had gone berserk!)

"*COUGAR'S GONNA CHEW ON YOU!*"

Rogers leaped at the footlights — a two-hundred-pound cat, snarling and shaking the enemy between his teeth. The kids went wild. Ms. Snell stood behind the mike with her mouth open.

Where'd this kid come from? Lily thought, beating her hands together the same as everyone else. He hadn't done anything at practice but try to keep up. She had no idea! Franklin Rogers was a clown, a grossly overweight sensation. And she had to follow *him*!

For the first time in her sixteen months of cheerleading, Lily felt her knees turn spongy. "You're a pretty good gymnast," he'd said. She hadn't even thanked him.

Ms. Snell's voice cut through the excitement. "After the next tryout, we want you to mark your ballots. Please follow the instructions if you want your vote to count."

Lily wiped her palms on her shorts, took a deep breath. Across the stage where everyone waited, Franklin was getting all the pats and smiles. About a hundred hands were reaching out to congratulate him. "Go for it!" she'd said. There wasn't one person left on her side of the stage to encourage her. She pressed her lips together and waited.

"And now, last — though certainly not least — Lily Jamison!" *Good old Snell!*

Lily plunged into her back handspring behind the curtain. Her legs and white boots flashed out of the wings a fraction ahead of the rest of her. Down and over. Again! And again! Twist and flip, finish with the splits. Arms spread, she treated them to a breathless smile.

The bell rang.

Lily waited. If anyone clapped, she couldn't hear it. *Damn the bell!*

Afterward, the auditorium buzzed. They were rattling their ballots, talking. Why didn't they shut up? Lily threw an anguished look at Ms. Snell.

"Your attention, please! We're not finished!"

Lily got to her feet, beginning the pattern of disco moves that introduced her cheer.

Someone laughed in front of the auditorium. Swiveling closer to the footlights, Lily gave them a hip thrust, then another. Laughter rippled back through the student body. Someone let out with a whistle. Shushing followed. Lily blinked back the tears. *God, they're rude!*

Suddenly she couldn't go on with the disco bit. The footlights blinded her. The rumble of conversation distracted her. She was alone, exposed, and she'd forgotten the words. All she could think of was the basic cougar yell, and that didn't have anything to do with what she'd planned.

"Go for it!" It was Franklin's voice, reaching her from the wings, and it broke the paralysis. Lily leaped into the air, making a C with her profile. "Give me a C!" she yelled.

"*Ceeeeeee!*" A dozen voices answered.

"Give me an O!"

"*Oooooooo!*"

"Give me a C-O-U!" She punched the air with angry fists.

Finally, Ms. Snell joined in from the mike, coaxing the students with both hands.

Somehow Lily got through it, her voice cracking on the *G-A-R*, applauding herself wildly at the end so *someone* in the vast auditorium would be clapping.

She cartwheeled off the stage—with perfectly controlled cartwheels. She could have gone on and on—up the aisle, into the hall, out the east door, four miles home. Cartwheels! Perfect circles, perfectly executed.

The curtains closed. Snell's frantic voice pierced the hubbub, giving directions.

Then Cory was hugging her, saying she was terrific. Franklin Rogers' face was at her own, red and smiley, his mouth working. Suddenly she wanted to scream. Afraid it would happen, she rushed back to the dressing room ahead of everyone else and ripped off her red silk blouse.

She wouldn't come back. The Clarkson Cougars would have to get along without Lily Jamison! She'd never come back! Lily was out of the building before the students were out of the auditorium.

Six

The fog had intensified, moving into Oak Grove from the valley below—a silent, rolling oppression that Daniel had watched all the way home from the university. The weather matched his mood. Mrs. Jamison's frantic phone call, which woke them after midnight, had plagued him through three classes and a lab. "Have any of you seen Lily?" she'd asked. "She never came home from school today."

Now, nearing three o'clock Tuesday afternoon, Daniel pulled into his driveway with Lily uppermost in his mind.

Grandma Perry met Daniel at the door. Her old face had been crisscrossed with wrinkles for years, but new worry lines creased her forehead today. "They haven't found her yet," she said, her hands pulling at her apron.

Skipper jumped up from the TV and scooted in between them. "How come Lily ran away?"

Grandma Perry shushed him with both hands, though she wasn't a lot bigger than he was. "Hush up now! I need to tell Daniel."

"But won't she never come back?" Skipper asked.

"Hold on!" Daniel set Skipper in a chair, loaded him down with two heavy books and a gym bag, then turned back to Grandma Perry, who was making big motions toward the Walker-Nelsons'.

"Lily's mama asked if you and that other girl... the girl down the street..."

"Erica?"

"Yes, Erica. She wants you two to walk up that canyon and holler around for Lily. I don't 'spose you'll find her, but the folks over there are worried sick."

"Okay." Daniel nodded. He was glad to be doing something. He sent Skipper upstairs with his gear, then walked back through the doorway. "I'll stop at the Jamisons' first, Grandma, to see if there's any news."

It didn't fit, somehow, Lily running away. She was so conventional. *Wasn't she?* She always did the expected thing. She worried about her grades, she was never late, never careless, someone you could depend on. But maybe she hadn't gone off of her own free will. How well did he know her anymore? He hadn't been close to Lily for a whole year.

A few minutes later, Daniel was standing in the Walker-Nelsons' entry hall, waiting for Erica.

"Do they think she's out in this fog?" Erica asked as she snapped up a denim jacket and tied on a bandanna.

"They don't know. She just disappeared. No one's seen her since yesterday at school."

Erica sat on the living room steps to pull on her boots. "Have they reported to the police and everything?"

"Mr. Jamison's doing that now. I guess they thought Lily would show up... you know, sooner or later."

Daniel and Erica took off around the house toward the barn. Erica stopped at the rear porch, flipped on a set of yard lights, then hurried to catch up with Daniel.

"Lily's been acting funny lately, if you ask me."

Daniel agreed.

[47]

"Have you seen her? Since we were swimming over there?"

"Nope. She's avoiding me."

"Me, too. She's been riding to school with her dad. Never once called to see if I wanted to go along. That's kinda arrogant, wouldn't you say?"

Daniel helped Erica open the gate. Lily wasn't arrogant. She was too sensitive, if anything. He suspected he and Erica had hurt her feelings plenty that afternoon at the pool.

The barn loomed out of the fog ahead of them, looking more like a hotel than a horse shed. It amused Daniel to have the acquaintance of horses who lived in such elegance.

"Man, this is the place to hide out!" he said, keeping his voice low. "If a person had food."

"That wouldn't bother Lily, would it?"

Daniel stopped as they neared the side door. "Wait a minute, Erica. What do we say if she's in there?"

Erica gave Daniel an exasperated look. "You want to rehearse?"

"Yeah, I do. Let's rehearse. Maybe she doesn't want to be found."

"Bullshit!" Erica turned and walked boldly ahead of him.

Daniel hated himself for noticing her near-perfect rear end at a time like this, but Erica had her ways when it came to getting noticed.

"You here, Lily?" she yelled in a voice that filled the barn. The only horse in the stalls lifted its head.

"Lily!"

No answer.

Erica gave Daniel a spooky look, then indicated that he should check the ground floor. She started up a stairway to the hayloft.

Daniel walked around, peering into the dark corners of the stalls—nervously—hoping she wasn't there. He spent the rest of the time letting old Pillow Ticking nuzzle him with homecoming affection. The barn smelled good to Daniel, like green hay and manure. The Walker-Nelson annex was a great place for dropping in *or* dropping out.

"I'll bet you just wanted to see old P.T.!" Erica accused, coming down the ladder at the other end of the stalls.

Daniel grinned, "The barn was Mrs. Jamison's idea. I didn't think Lily would be here, did you?"

"Not really. She was always nervous around the horses."

Erica walked to stand beside Daniel, stopping to stroke the mare's nose herself. Daniel watched her face soften. She was great with horses, though she rode roughshod over people sometimes. He wasn't sure it was a good idea, having her out searching for Lily, her general compassion quotient being about zero, but they were already committed.

Later, working their way upstream above the cul-de-sac, they nearly lost one another in the heavy fog.

"Lileee!" they called every few minutes.

Every hundred yards or so they'd meet and make a foray into the scrub oak together, Erica beating the brush with a stick for some reason. Daniel shuddered to think they might actually run across a body.

"What if someone kidnapped her?" Erica asked when they finally reached the mouth of the canyon. "They wouldn't bring her up here."

"No, but if she was attacked... or raped or something... this was her territory, you know. Lily used to hike up to the Narrows all the time."

Erica found a rock to sit on. "I don't think she's up here."

Daniel remained standing, fighting off his private gloom. It was getting dark fast. And cold. They'd have to go back soon.

Lily would freeze spending the night out in this kind of weather.

Daniel zipped up his vest, rolled down and buttoned the sleeves of his flannel shirt.

"Lileeee!" He tried again.

The canyon was ominously still. Fog blanketed everything, including sound.

"Let's use our heads," Erica said, as if they hadn't tried that yet. "Supposing one of us wanted to run off. Where would we go?"

"*You* think like a girl..."

"That's a chauvinist remark!"

"No, really, where would you go?"

"I'd go to Vegas!" Erica burst out laughing. "I'd steal about five thousand bucks from my dad and try my luck on the roulette wheel."

Daniel shook his head. "You probably would."

"You see?" Erica taunted him. "You and Lily are more alike than Lily and me!"

She was right. Different sex, different age, different race... Lily was still more like him than like Erica.

Shoving his cold hands in his pockets, Daniel turned and looked up the canyon, wondering where he would go if he wanted to run away. There was a lot of privacy up there. Visibility now was twenty feet at most, but his mind's eye could see on up the twisting path to the second stream crossing, the Narrows, finally the meadow. Lily knew the terrain as well as he did.

Daniel turned abruptly. "Let's go." He and his dad would come back tonight with their big-beam flashlight. They could at least make it up to the Narrows. He'd set the alarm for three o'clock and study tomorrow before daylight. He'd have to. Physics here wasn't any easier than it had been at Stanford.

Returning on the far side of the creek, Erica told Daniel how Lily had been at the tryouts, how she'd been laughed off the stage. Even *she* thought it was a kick—Miss Skin and Bones doing her disco thing right after the fat comedian.

"It was terrible timing," Erica said. "I felt sorry for her, you know, but she did look ridiculous."

Daniel felt his face burn. *God, no wonder she took off, if that's what happened!*

"Well, I think she's sick. Have you ever seen anyone so set on starving herself to death? Of course, she won't listen to me."

"Girls go on some really dumb diets. Maybe she's trying to look like a model. Or look like her mom."

"She's already skinnier than her mother." Erica stopped at the stream crossing and confronted him. "Why don't *you* say something to her? She'd listen to you, I bet."

Erica's compassion quotient jumped about twenty points on Daniel's scale. The puckering on her forehead reminded him of his grandmother's face. Suddenly Daniel felt like hugging her, like saying, "You're okay, you know that?" But he didn't. About four hundred years of taboos held him back.

Seven

Howard Jamison pulled into his driveway near nine o'clock that night, his eyes following the blunted beam of the car lights across the strip of lawn and onto the ornamental shrubs, which huddled in the night mist like ghosts. He was weary from looking, but his taut nerves wouldn't let him relax.

"Karen?" he called as he came in from the breezeway. He hung his coat, listening.

Then he heard Karen's step on the terrazzo of the dining-room floor and he went to meet her.

"Anything at all?" she asked.

He put his arm around his wife and led her toward the family room. "I talked to everyone I could think of. Cory went with me. On the way home I stopped to see this heavyset kid named Franklin Rogers. He's supposed to be the last one she talked to."

"What did he say?"

"It was a dead end. The only thing he can remember was how she looked at him before he went onstage. She said, 'Go for it!' He does remember that."

"'*Go for it!*' Oh Howard, what are we going to do?"

"The police have an all-points bulletin out with her description, though they didn't want to do anything until tomorrow. It

[52]

would sure help if we knew what she was wearing." He ran his hand through his hair, then loosened his tie. "What's the matter with us? She rode to school with me yesterday and I couldn't tell this police sergeant if she was in a skirt or pants. Fix me a drink, Karen."

He sank heavily onto the sofa, closing his eyes. "Make it stiff," he called after her.

Karen's voice reached him from the bar at the other end of the dining room. "That poetry we found in her wastebasket...do you think it means anything?"

"'Might I but moor tonight in thee'..." Howard Jamison repeated one of the lines under his breath. "Not to me it doesn't."

Karen entered the room and handed him the Bourbon and water. "If she did come home Monday while I was gone," she said, "how would we know? Her room's in perfect order, the way it always is. She could have changed clothes, taken money. How would we know?" When he didn't answer, Karen went back to wringing her hands.

Finally she walked to the double French doors and peered out. She pulled the drapes. She repeated the process on the other side of the fireplace. When she sat down on the edge of the coffee table, she faced him, their knees touching. "Daniel and Paul are up in the canyon now. They said they'd go as far as the Narrows if they could."

"Paul's looking for her, too?"

She nodded. "They've been marvelous. Florence came home from work, stayed here all afternoon."

"I know. I talked to her on the phone while you were lying down."

"If...*when*," Karen corrected herself, "Lily comes home, we're taking her to a doctor."

"Hasn't she been seeing Dr. Snyder? I thought she was going in once a week."

"I let her talk me out of it during tryouts."

"Hell, Karen, is cheerleading more important than her health?"

"*She* thinks so."

"Aren't *you* her mother?"

"Howard!"

"You're so damned preoccupied, Karen!"

"*I'm* preoccupied! You're the one who didn't know what your own daughter was wearing yesterday. I'd have noticed."

"You'd have noticed, all right, and commented. Lily changes two, three times some mornings to suit you. Of course, you weren't even up when she left."

"That's not fair. You know she's been going early. I get up with Juju"—she swung away from him and got to her feet—"whom you haven't even missed tonight."

He stared at what was left of his drink. "I know where she is. Florence told me she's spending the night with them."

Karen didn't say anything. She just stood there, hands in the pockets of her sweater, her mouth in a tight line.

"Look, Howard," she said, her voice softening, "I'm not suggesting we go back to Dr. Snyder with Lily."

"What are you suggesting?"

"I think...perhaps...she should see a psychiatrist."

"A psychiatrist! What for? She's losing weight, she's not losing her mind!" He stood to refill his glass.

"How can you be so sure?" Karen followed him to the bar and watched him pour a double shot. "I talked with Ms. Snell on the phone this morning. She thinks Lily's disturbed. Florence agrees. 'There's more going on with that diet than just taking off pounds,' she says. And I think they're right."

Howard shook his head. "That's the trouble with kids nowadays. They're hauled off to a headshrinker at the first little twinge in their psyches. Tell me, Karen, what's so hard about growing up in a household where everything's plentiful? Food? Clothes?

Spending money? We never had it so good, and we made it. I think Lily's spoiled. That's the whole problem. She's had too much."

Karen brushed a strain of gray-blond hair out of her face. "I've been telling myself it's just a phase. You know how easy she's always been. You used to say she was *born* adult, remember? Now, suddenly, she's hateful...and withdrawn...especially with me."

"You haven't thought it through, Karen. You know how people talk when they find out someone's seeing a psychiatrist. You know what her friends would say."

"What friends? She hasn't been on the phone with anybody for weeks. That can't be normal."

"Hell, she's not that messed up!" He added ice to his glass. "My daughter does *not* need a psychiatrist. After tonight, *I* may."

"Howard, you're never around her anymore. How would you know anything about her mental state?"

"Drink this"—he handed her the wineglass he'd filled with sherry—"and don't say one word about calories. You're going to get some sleep tonight."

"You're not listening." She clutched herself across the chest, backing away from him and the glass he held out to her. "You never listen," she repeated.

Slowly, elaborately, he poured the sherry into the bar sink. "We're not too good at that in this house, are we?...When's the last time you really listened to Lily, huh? Last time you two had a good chat? Tell me!"

"Will you stop shouting?"

"*I'm not shouting!*"

"Then lower your voice!" She walked away from him, ending their arguments the way she always did.

Howard Jamison finished his drink alone, sitting at the dining-room table. He pulled off his tie, unbuttoned the top of his shirt.

"God, I'm tired," he said, though no one was there to listen. "I'd better change clothes...go on up the canyon. If Lily's out there somewhere..."

He heard Karen in the kitchen fussing with the coffee maker. "What are you doing?" he called out to her. "You want to sober me up before the liquor has a fighting chance?" He put a finger on his lips. "Oh, sorry, sorry! I gotta *lower my voice*. Stay in control. Like *she* does."

He smiled at Lily's empty chair, as if she would comfort him if she were there. "How do you lower your voice when you're insane with worry? Explain that to me. Maybe I have something to yell about!"

He took the last swallow of Bourbon, unaware that his face had already collapsed.

"LILY!" he bellowed, suddenly perverse. "WHERE ARE YOU?" He smacked the glass down on the table, then strode out to the foyer and on to the double front doors, throwing them open to the night.

"LILEEEE!" he called "GODDAMN IT, LILY, WHERE HAVE YOU GONE?"

Quickly, Karen was beside him, pulling him back into the house and closing the doors. He let her hold him, let her arms contain the sobs that threatened to explode through his chest.

Then it was all over.

They recognized her voice at the same time, a small voice that sounded as scared as they were.

"I'm right here, Daddy."

Howard stiffened, yanking away from Karen. His eyes searched the dark at the top of the stairs.

"I've been here all along."

It was their Lily, standing at the balcony rail above them. Howard Jamison had her in his arms in less time than it took Karen to ask, *"Why?"*

Eight

"I'm Jessica Coburn," the doctor said as she came into the reception room. She extended her hand to Lily. "I'm very happy to meet you."

They shook hands, Lily smiling the best she could. She'd expected Dr. J. R. Coburn to be a man. Someone paunchy, like Dr. Snyder, or the pale, fidgety, horn-rimmed glasses type she'd seen on TV. Dr. Coburn was not only female, she was practically Lily's contemporary. How could *she* know anything?

"What a lovely shade of blue you're wearing!" the psychiatrist said as she closed the door to her office. "That color picks up your eyes, to borrow a line my old boyfriend used on me."

"Thank you," Lily said.

My mother dresses me, she wanted to say, *I'm her Barbie doll.*

"Won't you sit down?"

Lily sat down. Dr. Coburn was short. She probably couldn't bear looking up to a patient.

"Dorothy just brewed some fresh coffee. Would you like some?"

Lily shook her head no.

"We have Coke, Pepsi, 7-Up?" Her hands flipped around like they'd been choreographed. "How about a Tab?"

"No, thank you."

"All right...all right, you're forcing me to drink alone!" Coburn walked out, her heels noisy when she reached the adjoining room.

Lily took a deep breath, wiped her wet hands on her slacks. The university hospital had recommended Dr. Coburn for "persons with weight problems." Lily could see Coburn didn't have any weight problem of her own. A hundred and five, Lily guessed. In the jeans and cord blazer she wore, she could pass for a first-year teacher at Clarkson, or even a senior if you didn't look too close. Lily had expected someone older...uglier.

It wasn't any less scary, having her psychiatrist be a woman. The fact that Lily was here at all made her feel like some kind of nut. *When you see a shrink, you're either crazy or on the way. Everyone knows that!*

Lily looked around. Was it the coffee smell that made the room seem familiar? Or was it because she'd been "on the couch" so many times in Snell's office? There was a cascading plant hanging in one corner. Snell had a plant, too, named Calypso, but it was always struggling to survive. There were two other chairs in this room, one lumpy and slip-covered in giant red hibiscus. Lily sat on the only straight-back. There was no couch anywhere.

She studied the paneled wall opposite her that held about a thousand books. *The Listening Process.* Dr. Snyder sure hadn't read that one! *Family Therapy in Clinical Practice.* Next to it, *Psychotherapeutic Approaches to the Resistant Child.* Lily made a face.

Hey, maybe the couch was concealed *behind* the bookcase. Press, whirrrrr, the analysis chamber! Lily shivered and pulled down the sleeves of her sweater.

Dr. Coburn began talking before she ever got back to her desk. "The important thing for us to do today is to get to know one another a little." Then she smiled this terrific smile that transformed her Orphan Annie face. Right off Lily had to admit that Jessica Coburn, with her curly cut and big glasses, was not going to believe the same things she'd been telling Dr. Snyder. Lily watched her pull pencils out of a leather container, place them alongside a yellow legal-size pad.

"I doodle," she explained, making with the hands again. Then she leaned back in her chair and waited. It was Lily's turn.

"I don't think I need to be here," Lily said.

Dr. Coburn nodded. "But your mother... your parents... feel otherwise."

"I guess so. I'm here."

"I think you should know at the outset that you're not stuck with me... or the university clinic. You won't be locked into a counseling situation you don't need or can't tolerate. Also, you might feel better knowing I'm a lot older than I look. Now, that's my disclaimer. What's yours?"

Lily hesitated, not sure what she meant by "disclaimer." She looked down at her hands. "I guess... my mother has been listening to *Miz* Snell at school."

"And what does she say?"

"She says everyone needs a shrink. Except her. She'd like to be sitting where you are."

"What does Ms. Snell teach?"

"Dance. Gymnastics."

"Well"—Coburn took a sip of coffee—"I might like to trade places with her. Are you in the dance program there?"

"No."

"Gymnastics, then, I assume."

Assume what you like.

"You're built like a gymnast. How much do you have to work out?"

"I *was* in gymnastics for two years. Snell wouldn't sign me up this year."

"Why not?"

Look her straight in the eye came the voice of Lily's monitor.

"She wanted me to help with the sophomore cheerleading squad. It's a new program at Clarkson."

"I see. Sounds like a lot of responsibility."

Lily shrugged.

"Why is your mother anxious about you? Why would she want you to come in for counseling?"

Careful. She's zeroing in. "Why don't you ask her?"

"Her opinion may not be the same as yours. Yours is the one that counts here with me."

Lily caught herself fingering the fringe on her sweater belt. She stopped at once, lifted her chin. "I suppose she'd say I disgraced the family this week. And myself."

"That bad, huh?"

Lily smiled. "You know how mothers are," she said. Applause sounded in her head: *Keep to the generics!*

"What happened?"

"I hid out for a couple of days. They couldn't find me."

"Really? Where'd you go?" The doctor was interested now. She rolled her chair forward, rested her arms on the desk.

Lily took her time, telling about the tryouts, about cutting classes afterward, running the four miles home. She explained how she'd gone out to the hideout on the stream, not planning anything, just wanting to avoid her mother's questions when she returned from the city. Later she heard Juju calling her, and the whole thing turned into hide-and-seek. She had crept upstream, keeping out of her little sister's range.

"After dark I got scared. I knew they'd make me eat dinner if I went home. And I'd have to explain everything. It was easier just to sit there, but I got awful cold."

"Weren't you hungry?"

"I never get hungry."

"Oh..."

"Later, my folks went out in the car. I guess they were looking for me." Lily stopped short. She'd turned the session into a talk-athon, something she hadn't meant to do.

"And then? Don't leave me in the dark... so to speak," the doctor said.

"Well"—Lily crossed her legs—"I went back to the house. I could see Juju through the family-room windows watching TV with Trinh. That's the neighbor girl who baby-sits sometimes. So I just slipped back into the house. They didn't even know I was there."

"You stayed hidden all the next day?" Jessica Coburn rolled the pencil between her hands, her coffee sitting there like a forgotten prop.

"There's a supply closet in my mom's studio. I slept there. It's one place where Juju's not allowed to be. The next day—well, I got to liking it." Lily's mouth twitched. She hated that, when her mouth twitched all by itself.

"You were very definitely a missing person.'"

"I was missing long before that," Lily muttered.

"You don't mean physically missing?"

Lily held back at what sounded like a leading question. "I was just talking. It sounded good."

Long silence. Then Coburn took another tack. "Were you aware, Lily, of how your parents felt when they couldn't find you? Or were you so preoccupied with your own feelings that you didn't really think of them?"

"No, I knew how they felt. I tried not to think about them... or me. I didn't really plan it, you know, I just did it."

"You had a lot of hours alone. How did you occupy your mind all that time?"

"In the hideout I had my poetry book and was memorizing Emily Dickinson. We learn eighty lines if we want an A."

Coburn smiled, rested her chin on her hand. "Oh, Lily, you

take me back. I loved Emily Dickinson when I studied American literature. Did you learn all eighty lines?"

"More like a hundred and four."

"The soul selects her own society..." Coburn began.

"...then shuts the door." Lily finished the line.

"I guess that's what you were doing, those two days."

Lily hadn't thought of it that way. No wonder she hungered after the poet, whose quaint, drab life seemed a bright intensity next to her own! It was as if Emily Dickinson had written the lines for *her*. Lily smiled, letting down her guard for one moment.

"The morning of the second day," Coburn continued, "you said you spent it crouched in the shower, listening to your mother, who was outside calling you. How did you feel at that time?"

"I guess"—Lily's face grew warm—"I guess it gave me a feeling of power."

"How do you mean?"

"Well, you know..." Lily slipped her hands under her legs on both sides. "I could have opened the window and told her where I was."

"Were you tempted to do that?"

"I don't know. I *could* have, but I didn't."

"Then, later, when your friends were out looking for you, you actually stood at your bedroom window and watched them."

"For a minute. It was foggy. But I could hear them calling my name for a long time."

"Did you feel less comfortable having them search for you?"

Lily looked down at her knees. She was mortified, that's all.

"You know, Lily"—Dr. Coburn broke into her thoughts—"your dropping out for a couple of days isn't what worries me. That might have been healthier acting-out than it would appear. The fact that you felt you were 'missing'—in quotes—long before that might be more important. I think you're wise getting counseling now."

Lily gave Dr. Coburn a straight look. "It's strictly my mother's idea, not mine."

"The best time to see a psychotherapist is before you start babbling, right?"

The telephone buzzed then, and Lily guessed that her time was up.

"Yes, Dorothy. Right. Offer him a Coke or something. I'll be ready in a minute."

Lily stood and put on the camel dress coat her mother had suggested she wear, relieved beyond words to have her confessional over with. Proud of herself, too, considering she'd been so bitchy about coming.

"One minute, Lily. I need your weight, height, your family doctor's name before you take off. Routine stuff I should have taken care of first." She moved around the desk to help Lily off with her coat again. "Scale's in that supply room. Along with the brooms, soda pop, mice, and everything else. So watch your step."

Lily hesitated. "I can tell you what I weigh, Dr. Coburn."

"Let's check anyway."

"I weigh myself every morning."

Dr. Coburn still had her hand out for the coat but dropped it, tilting her head to one side. She "tsk-tsk'd" a few times.

"Our scales meet exacting Toledo standards. Yours are prejudiced. Come on, you can weigh yourself."

Clipboard in hand, Dr. Coburn led Lily into the "inner sanctum," as she called it.

"What's that for?" Lily pointed to a cot at one side of the cluttered room, curiosity usurping her manners. She knew there'd be a couch somewhere.

"That's for me. Occasionally I hide out, too."

So Coburn liked to share secrets with patients. *I, too, hide out from my mother.* Lily hoped she wouldn't barf.

She removed her shoes and got on the scale. Dr. Coburn rested the height bar on her head. "And in this corner...Jousting Jamison herself, standing five feet, seven inches tall, weighing in at ..." She waited as Lily pushed the two balance weights into place.

"...ninety-six and one half," Lily said, sounding pleased.

Dr. Coburn peered past Lily's shoulder. "You sure?"

"See?"

Coburn wrote it down, but her eyebrows still showed astonishment.

"Now. Your family doctor's name."

"Bart Snyder. He's in the Oak Grove Medical Complex."

Coburn wrote that down, too, then returned to her office, where she handed Lily her coat when she appeared.

"Will you be back?" she asked. "I think you ought to locate that missing person."

Lily put on her "wan smile," as her mother called it, but she didn't answer. She wanted out of there fast.

She walked past the Dorothy person, another patient, and on through the reception room without turning her head. How did *she* know if she'd be back? Her mother would be very disappointed, she could bet on that. Not once did Jessica Coburn tell her she had to eat more!

Nine

Lily broke lettuce into a large glass bowl, then added the cauliflower and salad tomatoes. Juju and Skipper sat at the kitchen counter with their sandwiches, watching her.

"The mushroom is the elf of plants," Lily quoted, thinking how much she appreciated the low calorie content of the pale vegetable.

"I don't like those things," Skipper said.

Lily looked up from the cutting board. "That's why you guys are eating peanut butter and jelly. Need something else? Potato chips?"

Skipper nodded yes, making big eyes.

"Potato chips are junk food, you know," Lily admonished, adultlike, but she reached into the cupboard anyway.

"I like junk food," Skipper said solemnly.

Juju giggled, pushing her plate toward Lily. "Give me some junk food, too."

Lily counted out exactly five chips apiece. She was glad she'd quit poisoning her system with salt and grease and all the other snack crap. The salad she was making for dinner was not only nutritious, it also added up to a mere forty calories per serving, including the lemon juice.

"You plan Saturday night dinner," her mother had told her that morning before she'd dropped her off at the psychiatrist's.

They were being so nice, using every wile to please her, to get her back to stuffing herself again. Well, it wouldn't work. Her mom's face fell flat when she said she'd like baked halibut and cold beets for dinner.

"Sounds delicious to me," her mother had said, though Lily didn't believe her. "Your father can't get by on that," she'd added in the next breath. "I'll fix a casserole for him."

Even though the meal fell within her calorie limits, Lily was dreading the ordeal of eating it with them. "We'll have a good talk tonight," her dad said when he left at noon to play tennis. And then the subtle way her mother fed Juju and Skipper early —"So they can watch TV. Skipper's sleeping over, you know." Lily wasn't fooled.

"Can I show Skipper where you hid?" Juju asked, licking jelly off her palm. "He wants to see."

Lily gave her a sharp look as she tossed the salad.

"Can I, huh?"

"Aren't you going to watch that Muppets special?"

"Yeah!" Skipper bounced on the stool, communicating his excitement to Juju.

Lily marveled at the attention span of five-year-olds. *That fast* the studio closet lost out to Miss Piggy.

Upstairs in her room, Lily changed into her warm-ups and hooded sweatshirt. Sitting on the window seat to tie her shoes, she was able to check the weather and Daniel's whereabouts at the same time. She could nearly see the front of the Perrys' house now; another week and all the leaves would be on the ground, giving her a clear view of his bedroom window. She remembered how bleak she'd felt last year when no yellow light ever appeared in those two rectangles. Now, sometimes, he was up studying until one or two in the morning. The night he'd been out looking for her she'd sat there in the dark past midnight, refusing to go to sleep until she knew he was home and in bed.

No matter. She didn't want to see him today. She had half a pound to take off before she could talk to Daniel again. She thought of the Saturday afternoon at the pool when Daniel and Erica had made such rude comments about her not eating. Alone in the house after her binge, she'd cried until her face was swollen.

When it was over, she'd looked in the mirror at her bloated and repulsive image. She'd finished the blueberry pie, the end of a roast beef, made herself a sandwich and a malt more chocolatey than any of Juju's. How could she have done it? How could she have let them ruin her discipline? Damn Erica. It was her fault!

She'd been so sick afterward, finger down her throat, bringing it all up, the bilious blue vomit stinging her nostrils. Immediately she'd slapped a fine on herself: *five more pounds!* Lily Jamison wouldn't see or communicate with Daniel until she'd done penance for that Saturday binge.

By skipping lunch the week she worked with the sophomores, she'd dropped two pounds. Her forced fast while hiding out Monday and Tuesday had nearly brought her to her goal. *Imagine, two pounds in as many days!* Lily grinned. *I should disappear more often.*

By running before dinner and doing calisthenics at bedtime, she might get rid of a few more ounces. If all went well, she could see Daniel next week.

Lily did her warm-ups before leaving her room. She rotated her head, her shoulders, sat on the floor touching nose to knee. She was beginning to feel good again—lean, strong, clearheaded—for the first time in two weeks.

She could face them at school Monday. Ninety-six pounds of confidence, she'd plainly be in control again. Cory and the others—they'd undoubtedly wallowed all week in their delicious gossip about her, snouts together like hogs at a trough. She could hear Snell now: "It's none of my business, but is your doctor using a Freudian approach?"

"No," Lily would say, "she's using the friendly approach."

However, it wasn't Snell's face, but Jessica Coburn's, that danced ahead of her as she left her room to go running. Lily knew that a psychiatrist specializing in "eating disorders" wasn't going to sit around reciting Dickinson forever. Sooner or later, her shrink would be forcing food on her. And if she wanted to stay thin, which was more important than anything, she'd have to find a way to get around Coburn. Maybe she could convince her parents they were wasting their money—that her doctor was too young or too inexperienced or something.

The doorbell rang just as Lily reached the bottom of the stairs. She frowned. With Juju outside playing, she'd have to answer it herself.

"Grandma Perry!" Lily exclaimed at the door.

Wearing a raspberry-colored suit and pillbox hat, Daniel's grandmother was obviously dressed for a visit. She also came bearing a gift wrapped in foil.

"Hello there," she said, smiling up at Lily. "Is your mama home?"

"No, she's downtown. She had to deliver some work to Dorbach's, but she'll be back before long."

Grandma Perry's shoulders sagged with the news. Her smile was fast disappearing, too.

Lily hesitated only a second. "Look...I'm here. Can't you come in for a while?" Of all the people she knew, Grandma Perry was the easiest to entertain. She wouldn't stay long. Besides, Lily could relate to her disappointment. "Come on in, Grandma Perry. I can make coffee just as well as my mother can."

"Oh, dear, I'm afraid I'm interferin' with your plans." Her

large eyes were full of apologies as she steadied herself at the doorframe, but when Lily continued to insist, she stepped in. "Your mama especially invited me to come visitin' this afternoon, but I suppose she got busy and forgot. Here"—she handed Lily the loaf-shaped package she was carrying—"this is for you, fresh out of the oven. You can share it with the folks if you've a mind, or eat it up all by yourself."

"Ooh, thank you! It smells so good. What is it?"

Grandma Perry scrunched up her shoulders. "Applesauce cake," she said, sounding pleased. "Been my favorite for years."

They started toward the kitchen together, Lily's hunger piqued by the spicy aroma of the warm loaf in her hands.

"We'll sit right here in the breakfast nook, Grandma Perry. Now, I can't remember, are you a cream-and-sugar person?"

"Oh, yes, I'm a big nuisance." She settled herself happily on a chair. "You'd think I'd get with the program, wouldn't you?"

Lily grinned as she filled the coffee maker and set some mint wafers on a plate. She loved listening to Daniel's grandmother. Her blend of southern accent and poor grammar, sprinkled with Daniel's phrases, made her a genu*ine* Oak Grove original.

"What's been ailin' you?" Grandma Perry asked straight out as soon as Lily sat down opposite her. "You've been losin' flesh ever since summer. Pretty thing like you..." She reached over and patted Lily's hand. "We've all been worryin' about you. Florence thinks you may have a touch of—what's it called? Anex*o*ria? I sure hope you don't have that."

Lily laughed at Grandma Perry's mispronunciation. "No," she said reassuringly, "I don't have *that*. Actually, I've been trying to lose weight. I'm not sick." It was flattering that the Perrys would be so concerned about her. "Say," she couldn't wait to ask, "how's Daniel? I haven't seen him since the day after he got home."

"Oh, my, that Daniel. He's another one I worry about."

"You do? How come?" Lily asked, watching the tiny woman stir huge amounts of cream and sugar into her coffee.

"I don't think that boy's studyin' what he's cut out for. Never saw anyone work so hard and enjoy it so minimal." She made a sudden slurping noise, for which she immediately apologized amid much napkin fumbling and dabbing. "Old people shrink up," she told Lily confidentially, "and that includes the gums. Gives my false teeth too much room for rattlin' around. It's very embarrassin' in polite society."

"Please, enjoy yourself. I'm not polite society, not me."

Tasting her own coffee, Lily tried to remember the last time Daniel's grandmother had come visiting. It had been ages. She'd brought gingersnap cookies that time. "You're looking very pretty today," she said suddenly, "but I hope you didn't get all dressed up to visit us."

Grandma Perry reached up to adjust her hat, her smile broadening. "It's my birthday. I figured I'd just put on the dog for once."

"Your birthday! Why didn't you tell me?" How awful that her mother had forgotten! Lily was on her feet at once, taking Grandma Perry's face in her hands, kissing her noisily on the cheek. "It's *your* occasion, so you baked *me* a cake. Wow, am I honored! Which birthday is this, or aren't you telling?"

"Sure I'm tellin'." Her crinkled face lit up. "I'm seventy-nine Big Ones. And every year has been better than the last."

Lily's laugh rippled out. "You honestly mean that, don't you?"

"Cross my heart. If spared, I'll be havin' such a good time at one hundred they'll have to lock me up for disturbin' the peace."

They both fell apart over that. Then Daniel's grandmother told Lily about getting a corncob doll on the first birthday she could remember. She was three, and her folks were still share-cropping at the time. She went on to tell Lily about other unforgettable birthdays, including the "humdinger" when she turned sixteen and her brother put a blow snake in her bed.

Before Lily knew it, her mother's car was in the driveway and she realized her chance to run before dinner was gone. It surprised her that she didn't even care. Celebrating with Grandma Perry had positively transformed her day!

Dinner hour that night started out better than Lily had expected, too. Her dad was in a really terrific mood when he came home. He'd had some drinks at the Racquet Club and was feeling no pain. In fact, he pulled Lily down on his lap in the family room and called her his tomboy, something he hadn't done for ages.

"What's this tomboy doing on my lap?" he teased. "Didn't I bump you off my knees about six years ago? You must be going backward or something."

Lily snuggled up to him. There were times when she liked being a little girl again. "Goo-goo, ga-ga," she gurgled, acting silly, looking at her father through a strand of hair she pulled over her eyes. He chuckled, bounced her up and down on his knees.

"Dinner's getting cold," Karen sang out from the dining room.

"Don't tell her," Lily's dad whispered, "but I'm not even hungry."

"Me either."

Reluctantly, Lily stood and they went into the dining room together.

Seeing the table set with a cloth and centerpiece, Lily knew her hunch had been right. Tonight's dinner was supposed to be special.

"Clinched a deal today!" her dad announced as Karen served the halibut.

"That's marvelous!" Mrs. Jamison said. "What kind of deal?"

"Gregorson signed for the Quailbrook Apartments."

"What's so great about that?" Lily asked.

"Forty units? It's like making a year's salary in one afternoon. I beat him at tennis, besides, which was hardly a sound tactic on my part."

Lily studied the small filet on her plate as her father talked on. She pressed the butter out of it with her fork. She'd wanted it baked, not broiled. With her dad in such a good mood, maybe she could get by eating only half of it. She'd eat both small beets. And the salad.

"Lily, your mother's talking to you."

She looked up.

"How was it?" her mother wanted to know.

Lily spread her napkin. "I haven't tasted it yet."

Her mother smiled. "I'm talking about your visit to Dr. Coburn, not your halibut."

It was private, she wanted to say. "It was a pain," was what came out. "I hated it!"

"Oh, Lily"—the face went all motherly for a minute—"I didn't want to subject you to a bad experience."

"What did I tell you?" her father was quick to add.

"Didn't you like her?" her mother persisted. "She has a marvelous reputation. Florence Perry says we were very lucky to get an appointment with her."

If her mother used that word one more time Lily thought she'd puke. *Marvelous* was the phoniest of words, Karen Jamison's catchall expression that described everything from her husband's rip-off real estate to a Givenchy gown. If Coburn was marvelous, Lily could do without her.

"Did she put you on a special diet?" her father asked.

"Diet?" Lily looked right through him. "I'm already on a diet."

"A diet is a *proscribed* set of foods." He sounded annoyed, cutting his fish with more vigor than was necessary. "Some diets are for gaining weight, you know."

"We didn't talk about diet."

"She didn't notice that you"—her dad stopped, gesturing toward her with his knife—"that you need to put on a little weight?"

"I'll bet she doesn't weigh any more than I do." Lily tasted the fish, giving them a cool, triumphant look. "The halibut's marvelous," she said, "but I wish you hadn't added the butter."

She nearly choked on the adjective she'd just used. She'd rather talk like Grandma Perry than end up sounding fakey like her mom. What was happening to her, anyway?

Ten

I wonder if she'll speak to me, Lily thought as she left for the bus stop Monday morning. She wouldn't blame Erica if she didn't. But there she was, waiting at the end of the Walker-Nelsons' long drive for Lily to catch up, waving like crazy.

It was a snapping cold morning. Their parkas were zipped up to their chins. Erica's red cheeks, her long hair bouncing out from under a fuzzy white cap made her look closer to twelve than seventeen. As always, she appeared to be popping with good news. Lily almost turned back. How could she stomach Erica after having a first-class fight over breakfast with her parents? She was *not* eating bacon and eggs anymore!

"Hi, Lily!" Erica swung into step beside her. "Guess what?"

"Give me a clue. I've been out of touch."

"Hey, that's right, you have." Erica gave her a long, analytical look. "You doing okay now?"

Lily shrugged.

"You know, I was laying bets you'd left town—gone to Vegas or L.A. But you were right here all the time. That's class! I mean, that's really cool." She grinned.

"I'm glad you understand."

"No kidding," Erica talked on, "I've felt like splitting lots of times."

"But you never did."

"Once. When I was little. My mother packed a suitcase for me. You know, that corny trick every mother pulls. She put in a box of Cheerios, all my favorite books, my toothbrush, and my teddy..." Erica laughed.

"What happened?"

"I couldn't lift the suitcase, so I made up with Mommy and stayed home."

Lily's 'mommy' would never have packed a runaway bag for her! She'd have enrolled her in Ultimate Nursery Experiences... or sent her to a kiddie shrink.

They were at the Oak Grove pillars now and Lily craned around to see if the bus was coming. The less time she had to spend with Erica the better.

"Listen, I have to tell you this!" Erica persisted.

"So tell me."

"John Hazeltine asked me to marry him last night."

"Erica!" Lily stared.

Erica dissolved in a giggling spasm. "I don't even like him much, let alone *love* him!"

"And he asked you to marry him?"

"He said he'd keep after me until I did." Erica's lips were pressed together in a smug line. Then she broke out laughing again. "It's so funny I had to tell you."

Lily didn't know what to make of it. John, a sophomore at the university, had dated Erica off and on for two years. He'd scared Lily to death the one time he'd come to their house to swim with Erica. He was a terrible flirt, had stroked Lily's arm, leg, whatever he could reach, but only when Erica was swimming underwater. He was so *overpowering*! She was sort of afraid of him. Afraid, too, of how he made her feel when he touched her.

[75]

She knew what the two of them did when they were alone at his house. Erica had told her. Actually, she couldn't imagine John being interested in marrying anyone.

"What did you say?" Lily asked finally.

Erica leaned close, her eyes wicked. "I asked if he was pregnant."

Lily had to laugh. "I can't believe you, Erica. Are you making this up?"

"I swear to God! He says his father wants him to get married, too, so he'll settle down and be serious about school. Is that choice enough?"

The bus arrived. The conversation ended. They had to separate, with Lily sitting near the front next to Eda Mae Rolphe, a girl in her English class. Without being asked, Eda Mae immediately began to fill her in on what she'd missed.

"We spent the entire week on the English Romantics," said Rolphe in her perfectly articulated speech. "Starting with Coleridge, 'The Rime of the Ancient Mariner,' which Mrs. Fairborne read all period...." Total recall was Eda Mae's biggest problem. She made straight *A*'s, the same as Lily, but that's all Eda Mae had going for her. If you ever made the mistake of asking her a question, you were flattened with information.

Eda Mae was just warming up when the bus stopped for the kids at the Pinebrook development. As they swung around into the parking area, Lily saw Franklin Rogers standing among the other Clarkson students. What was *he* doing at Pinebrook? He'd never ridden her bus before! Lily looked away. Were they doomed to be neighbors?

Suddenly, remembering tryouts brought blood to her cheeks. She felt a fist tighten inside her empty stomach. She hoped Porky Pig wouldn't notice her, but of course he did.

"Lily!" he exclaimed, like prophecy fulfilled. She had to look at him.

"Hi."

Eda Mae herself took a breather, glancing from one to the other.

"Hey, I got elected," Franklin told her. "I been wanting to tell you."

"Good for you."

Others were pushing in behind him. "Move it, Rogers!"

"Go around," he balked, leaning over Lily.

"I would if I could!"

General hilarity.

"They give me a hard time," he muttered, forcing Lily against Eda Mae. Suddenly Lily found herself face to face with Franklin's lapel button—"I'm a vampire. I can't afford to eat!"—and she started laughing.

"Sorry," Franklin said at her ear, hanging in between them to let everyone else pass. "You still gonna be our coach?"

"You don't need any help from me," she said.

"Aw, shucks, that's not true."

Rogers was tenacious in more ways than one, already talking over Eda Mae, who'd resumed with Coleridge, then gone on to Percy Bysshe Shelley in one long, unpunctuated sentence.

"I had this idea for a pyramid, see—"

"The recurrent theme in Shelley's poetry is love," Eda Mae perked on, "although a desire for death can be found in some of his lyrics. Mrs. Fairborne attributes this to the really weird life he led."

Franklin was gripping the bars of both seats—hers and the one ahead—lurching with the bus, detailing his big plans for the sophomore squad. His breath smelled exactly like a Reese's peanut butter cup. Eda Mae next to her was still spewing out data like a computer. Suddenly Lily needed air.

"Hey," she stopped Franklin, "let's talk later, okay?" He caught on at once when she hooked her thumb in Eda Mae's direction.

"Sure." Then he reached in his coat pocket and pulled out a lapel pin for Lily. "Wear it," he said. "It's a Rogers original."

He walked toward the back, exchanging cuffs with the guy behind Lily who'd been whispering "pork belly" all the time he'd been standing there.

"Shelley was so romantic, Lily. He eloped with this girl who was only sixteen and off they went to deliver the Irish from tyranny!"

Lily examined the tiny lapel pin, which was no larger than her fingernail. "More is less," it said in a fine script, then "Think small" under that. Lily smiled. She clipped it on her parka. It was her kind of statement, even if it was endorsed by the Incredible Hulk.

Eda Mae was still at it as they filed off the bus. "Today we're reading 'Ode to the West Wind,' which I love!" *She's all pink and excited,* Lily thought, reminded of Erica and the way her eyes had snapped talking about John Hazeltine. Had they all flipped out over sex? All but her?

"Thanks for the review, Rolphe, but I've gotta get an *ad*mit." Lily hurried away. "See you and Shelley in class."

The ride had worn her out. She felt a dizzy headache coming on. Between fighting at home and pandemonium on the bus, she wasn't sure this day was going anywhere.

At the locker Lily stripped off her parka. She glanced down to see the slight rise of her nipples against the velour sweater. She was almost flat—sleek and svelte and *flat*! The five pounds had made a difference. She remembered Erica lecturing her at the pool one day: "You know you've lost too much when you put your bra on backward and it fits be؟ter!"

Lily gathered her books in her arms. *What bra?* she asked herself, pleased.

The note came for Lily during the sixth-period American Problems class, intruding on what had been almost a decent day. She had eaten lunch with the varsity cheerleaders, though it wasn't her idea. Cory caught her leaving the line with her tray, grabbed her from behind, and marched her straight to the table where they were sitting. The cheerleaders clapped, of all things! Even the three new squad members looked at her sort of reverently. Wendy and Jeanne said stuff such as, "We're really going to miss you," and "You had all the good ideas," and "I know it won't be the same this year." Carol leaned across the table herself and whispered, "It took a lot of guts to try out after you'd been sick. Everyone admires you."

She *hadn't* been sick.

"Snell wants you to travel with us, anyway," Cory told her, "act as an advisory person, something like that."

Sounds like a ton of fun! Lily thought sardonically. How could Snell ask her to be cloakroom attendant after she'd been cheerleader captain? She wouldn't do it!

As the sixth period crawled to a conclusion, Lily unfolded the note to read it again: "Meet me in the office after school. A mini-conference, please. Beverly Snell."

She stuffed the paper into her notebook and stared out the window, trying to imagine how furious Snell must have been with her last week. Mercifully, however, she couldn't concentrate on her teacher. She kept seeing Daniel's face, kept touching his cheek with her hand. There, in the privacy of her desk—with nothing more distracting than a page of print headed "Poverty Pockets in Appalachia"—Daniel and she took off running along Danish Road, laughing, their faces lifted to the sun. Afterward, they made their way uphill alongside the creek, talking, feeling close. They'd be holding hands, the way they had in the hideout saying good-bye. She wondered if it would ever happen again.

Of course, he was the only boy she'd ever allowed to touch her. And all of that was kid stuff, ducking and shoving at the pool, walking with their arms slung around one another. "My gal pal," Daniel used to say. Other guys had tried their strategies on her, but somehow she'd managed to keep away from the groping hands and the hot breath. Cory's big passion scene had come during cheerleader camp when he'd finally pinned her against the cabin rail for a good-night kiss. She'd tasted his lips for a whole day after, feeling somehow unclean. She remembered being greatly relieved, about Thursday of that week, when he discovered Carol was more his type.

Lily sighed. Leaning forward on her elbows, she tackled the poverty pockets for the third time in an hour.

"There you are, Lily!" Ms. Snell met her at the office door. "Welcome back to reality." Big gestures. Big smiles.

She closed the door at once, gave Lily a perfunctory squeeze. "You've really had a time, haven't you?" she said, shaking her head. She indicated the couch, filled two cups at the coffee urn, then sat down at the other end of the vinyl sofa herself.

Lily thought of Coburn's office and the same pervasive smell of coffee. Remembering other details, she turned to check the spider plant in the corner. "Did you water Calypso last week while I was gone?"

"No!" Snell jumped to her feet. "I didn't think of it." Biting her lip, she hurried to fill a paper cup in the adjoining bathroom. Lily smiled, feeling superior. She reminded herself she was *not* going to be talked into anything tonight.

Once the plant was watered and dripping, Snell sat down at her desk and started rummaging through a pile of papers. Lily had winced, watching Snell drown the scraggly plant she herself had coaxed back to health since September.

"I'm not angry with you for last week," Snell said for openers. "I know how disappointed you were and how hurt. You did put your folks through hell for a couple of days there, you know that..."

Lily nodded.

"...but I understand. I do understand."

Okay, okay, you understand!

"I have something I want you to see.... It's here someplace... if I can find it."

Lily thought she might be spared after all. Snell never found anything once it was filed in one of her stacks. Lily leaned back and sipped at the coffee, letting it warm her. It was time, she reminded herself, to break out the heavy sweaters and wool pants. Lately, she was always cold.

"Here it is!" Snell claimed victory, fishing out a newspaper clipping and spreading it in front of her. "Have you heard of this disease called anorexia nervosa?"

Lily didn't answer.

"Well, it's"—Snell spread her hands—"kind of a psychosomatic thing. Do you know what I mean?"

"I know what psychosomatic means." After all, she'd had one semester of psychology.

Snell adjusted her glasses. "I'm beginning to suspect you have anorexia."

Lily worked to keep from laughing at Snell's instant diagnosis. "Why do you think that?" she asked.

"By the amount of weight you've lost. The popular term for it, according to this article, is 'the skinny disease,' and in every case it begins with excessive dieting."

Oh, no, you're not going to undo all my hard work with scare tactics!

Lily sat forward. "I'm just getting where I want to be," she said, on the defensive after all. "I work very hard at maintaining my weight."

"And I appreciate that. You work hard at everything. I don't believe you ever slouched through a project in your life. But there's such a thing as going too far, Lily, and I think that's what you're doing with this diet. Anorexics don't see themselves as being thin. Someone has to tell them." She sat back, studying Lily's reaction, which was as stonily indifferent as Lily could make it. "I wouldn't be your friend if I didn't tell you how worried I am about you."

Lily looked beyond Snell, out of the window. Snell would probably make her miss the activity bus. She'd already ruined her plans for running immediately after school. Daniel had quit going out weekday mornings, had taken up an afternoon schedule instead; if she saw him this week, it would have to appear accidental. She gave Ms. Snell an icy look, but it didn't cool her enthusiasm one degree.

"A phys ed teacher has to make all kinds of things her business, Lily. Good heavens, I've even had to talk to guys about their foot odor because the coaches wouldn't. If I see a student having problems, I make it my business."

You can say that again.

"What about your periods? Have they stopped?"

Lily felt herself blushing. What was Snell driving at?

"Listen to this." Ms. Snell bent over the newspaper item, underlining words as she read them: "One of the consequences of extended undernutrition is the cessation of menses." Snell looked up. "That's when your period stops."

"What are you talking about? Why would I stop having periods?" Ms. Snell was disgusting! Why was she asking such a personal question?

"All right, Lily, I'm not trying to embarrass you. What have you eaten so far today?"

"I skipped breakfast," Lily said, starting out honest. "But I ate school lunch." She had eaten some of it. She'd promised her dad that morning to taste everything on her tray.

"All except the chocolate chip cookies," she corrected herself. "I'm not into desserts. I gave mine to Cory."

Ms. Snell looked skeptically at Lily. "Could you be having a thyroid problem?"

"Dr. Snyder says I'm healthy. I saw him only a month ago."

"Read this article anyway, Lily. Maybe you are beginning to eat properly. I hope so. You put on a dozen pounds, maybe fifteen, and we'll get you back in the gymnastics program in the second semester."

Some trade-off.

Lily accepted the clipping Ms. Snell thrust at her, at the same time observing the dark water stain on the carpet under the plant. Poor Calypso... overwatered, unable to reject the flood now bathing its roots. She, at least, could control her intake, though it was getting harder all the time. If it was up to Snell or her folks, she'd simply be a receptacle. Open the lid, pop in pork chops, apple pie with cheese, a cup of chocolate swimming with marshmallows, a dozen or so rolls. Push the button. *Chomp, chomp, grind...*

Lily stood and put her cup by the coffee urn. She felt light-headed. The room began to tilt. Quickly she sat back down again.

"I have plans for you, Lily. I'm not going to let your talents go to waste this year."

Like Eda Mae, Snell didn't notice anything when she was talking. Lily smiled down at her hands, waited for the dizziness to pass, then gathered up books and papers, stacking them neatly. She'd have to walk home now, she suspected. By the time she got back to her locker and outside, the bus would have gone.

"I was as distraught as your own mother last week, Lily. Tell her I appreciate the phone call when you finally...you know... showed up."

Lily stood. "Thanks, Ms. Snell. I have to go, really, or I'll miss the bus. Thanks for everything."

Back in the classroom wing, approaching her locker, Lily slipped Ms. Snell's clipping in the janitor's huge collector bin as she passed. Of course she'd read about anorexia! It was discussed in all the magazines. Besides, when that singer died of it, her mother had circled all the newspaper articles for her to read. What was wrong with Snell and her parents? She wasn't about to diet herself *to death*. She understood nutrition, knew what felt right for her. She wasn't stupid!

Lily packed a book and notebook into her day bag. She'd run the four miles home, the way she'd done it a week ago after tryouts. *If* she didn't develop a side stitch or cramps in her calves. She doubted if she'd see Daniel today, even from a distance.

Eleven

Lily wiped her hands on her jeans, rushing to catch the phone. *Always* it rang when she was in the middle of something.

"Jamisons."

She leaned against the wall when she heard his voice, making a face she was glad Franklin Rogers couldn't see.

"Right. It starts at seven."

"Well... just a minute... let me have a consultation." Lily held the phone against her stomach, her mind racing for an excuse. She walked the full length of the cord, then back. "I can *probably* pick you up, Franklin. No, don't walk over. I'll pick you up."

She nodded, listening to him carry on about not having his license yet. She glanced outside to check the weather, which had been threatening snow all day.

"Sure, no problem. What's your address?"

The buzzer sounded. "Hey, my cookies are burning. See you tonight, okay?"

Lily slammed the phone on the hook and dashed across the room to the oven. Was Rogers going to make a pest of himself? She'd die if Daniel ever saw her with Fat Franklin. It was bad enough to be hanging out with the sophomore crowd...

Lily slipped the ginger cookies off the sheet and arranged them on cooling racks. Shaped like footballs, the first batch was already decorated with icing. She still had to add the names of the sophomore cheerleaders to each giant cookie, then wrap them in plastic. She was glad she didn't have to eat one.

Lily remembered last year's initiation, how the varsity cheerleaders had made the juniors their "slaves" for a whole week. She'd loved it, tagging along after Kim Brewster, carrying her books, fetching her Cokes, waiting humbly at her locker to see what Kim wanted in her sack lunch the next day. Thinking about it now, Lily wondered how Kim kept her figure with such a gross appetite.

But this year Snell changed the initiation procedure, limiting activities to one Friday night, the only one that wasn't scheduled with games. Of course Snell had included her, suggesting that she bring dessert. Manipulating Lily had turned into a national pastime, all right.

Lily started to lick the icing off her fingers. *Don't taste!* her censor shouted. She looked at her hand in disgust, quickly wiped it on the dishcloth. Just today she'd broken ninety-three pounds. She thought of Dr. Coburn, who'd be pop-eyed tomorrow when she saw how much Lily had lost. She'd have to wear extra clothes ... maybe drink a lot of water... before going downtown to meet her shrink.

"My shrink," she said and chuckled, outlining a football with green icing. She ought to put Coburn's name on one and make her eat it!

It had just started to snow when Lily drove into the Pinebrook neighborhood to pick up Franklin. He was waiting on the porch, a tan garbage bag slung over one shoulder. He was wearing knickers and cross-country ski socks with big white snowflake patterns. She had to remind herself that he was talented. Otherwise, she was put off by his oddness and totally repulsed by his massive flesh.

Franklin started gabbing as soon as he got in the car. By the time they reached Clarkson she learned he'd been a junior high cheerleader in Denver, had just moved to Canyon City, was a history buff and a small-scale manufacturer of lapel pins.

"What does that one say, that you're wearing tonight?" she asked.

"'Pool it, don't fuel it,'" he said.

She laughed. "Well, that's what we're doing."

"Come on over sometime. I'll show you my operation. Of course, we just moved in, so I'm not totally set up."

"Do you sell those pins?" she asked.

"Yeah, I crank up for business every once in a while. Everybody likes slogans and campaign buttons. I handled a dental meeting once last year. The slogan wasn't much—'Open Wide, America'—but they wanted these big pearly teeth all around the perimeter. I thought it looked more like *Jaws*, but they loved it."

Lily turned into the student parking lot at school. *Too bad he's such a porker,* she thought. *He's sure full of surprises.*

The seniors were serving the spaghetti dinner that night for initiation, so, naturally, Lily volunteered to help serve instead of eat. After dinner, there was "torture time"—relays with raw eggs on the spoon—then a sardine contest between sophomores and the JV to see how many cheerleaders could stuff themselves into a refrigerator box in thirty seconds. Most of it was childish, Lily thought, from the lofty position of a has-been.

Then came the sophomore skit, whose sole purpose was to get Lily to say *yes.* Stephanie and Franklin had the leads in the melodrama, which was performed to organ music someone had taped. Dressed in tatters and rags (school colors, of course), Stephanie wept and wailed and wrung her hands, a very noisy damsel in distress.

> I *can't* learn to cheer,
> I *can't* learn to cheer,
> I *can't* learn to cheer aloooooooooone!

Franklin, swishing his black cape, skulked wickedly around the helpless girl.

> You *must* learn to cheer,
> You *must* learn to cheer,
> You *must* learn to cheer, you crooooooooone!

Finally, of course, Lily came to the rescue in the person of Jean Callaghan, the tallest, thinnest blonde on the sophomore squad, who was wearing Lily's very own monogrammed jogging suit, the one she'd used at school the week she'd spent drilling them.

The act was so corny, Lily had to laugh as hard as everyone else. When the messenger came in, furiously pumping his gold and green tricycle up to where Lily sat, it was to bring her a Western Union telegram. She had no choice but to say, "Yes, I'll be your coach."

Franklin was elated, telling Lily twice on the way home how glad he was that she'd be working with them. Normally, Lily would have been fuming at Snell's underhanded trick, but at the moment she had to concentrate on the driving. The storm had already put down a ton of snow. Visibility was zero, and the few cars on the street were creeping. The snow blew straight into the headlights, making it nearly impossible to find the right side of the road.

"Keep the window down on your side and watch for me," Lily

told Franklin. Then, halfway home, she herself got out and brushed off both windshields. To make matters worse, the snowplow had turned around at the bottom of Oak Grove Drive, and Lily was forced to stop. Neither Danish Road nor Oak Grove had been cleared.

"We can't get through," she said in a tight voice, checking her rearview mirror. "We don't have snow tires on yet. What'll we do?"

"I can call my dad from your house," Franklin said. "We've got a four-wheel-drive."

Lily let the engine run, not knowing what to do next, hating times like this when she couldn't make a decision.

"Your dad won't be mad at you, will he? Lock the car and we'll walk up the hill."

"You don't know them!" She wouldn't get the car again for a month if she had to leave it stranded. Why had she asked to drive the Buick, anyway?

"What else you gonna do?" Franklin asked.

She wished he'd shut up. It wasn't his car. He didn't know one thing about getting stuck and being responsible for it.

Finally Lily pulled the car around the corner, slid into the right-hand curb—the way she knew she would—and was forced to cut the engine. "Okay," she said, "now we have to walk."

Franklin made her hang onto his arm, which was a good thing because her sneakers were slippery. Immediately her shoes filled with snow, as did the open throat of her quilted vest. They were the odd couple, all right—slipping and sliding, a garbage bag of costumes banging against Franklin's left arm, Lily clinging to the other. It took all her strength to wade uphill through the snow.

Then they heard the shrieks and yells coming from the top of the street. "What's going on?" Franklin asked.

"Sounds like the kids are out in the circle." Suddenly things didn't seem so grim. Lily let go of Franklin. "They're having a snowball fight."

It happened every winter, the two or three times when the street was blocked off with snow. She and Daniel and Erica used to run the moonlight course on their sleds when they were little.

When they were close enough to see what was happening, Lily cringed. Daniel was going to see her with Franklin! In fact, he was right there, lobbing snowballs across the lighted circle at Erica's team.

"Kill 'em, kill 'em!" Juju chanted from Daniel's side.

Skipper and Trinh were whooping it up beside Erica.

It was too late for the shortcut, they'd already seen her. Lily ducked as the next bomb landed at her feet. "Our neighbors," she shouted to Franklin, feeling she had to explain, "and my bloodthirsty sister!"

"Truce, truce!" Erica waved her cap. Daniel tossed the next snowball overhead, letting it land behind him. The little kids groaned as Erica and Daniel converged on Lily. They hated a time-out.

"I'm stuck down below," Lily said right off, "in the new car, if you can believe it."

"Who's this?" Erica grinned at Franklin.

"Oh, excuse me. This is Franklin Rogers, one of the cheer-leaders. He lives over in Pinebrook."

"I'm Daniel, this is Erica." Daniel finished the introductions, then turned back to Lily. "Couldn't Franklin and I get you out?"

"I don't think so," she said, bending sideways to shake snow out of her hair.

"Not without snow tires," Franklin added. "She wouldn't make it on up."

"I've got a better idea than digging out Lily's car," Erica said. "Nobody's home at my house. Why don't you all come down and I'll make us some hot toddies?" Suddenly she was button-holing Franklin. "Hey, you old enough for a hot toddy?"

A gust of wind lifted Franklin's hair on top, making him look like an over-size cupid. "I could go for one," he said, his fat cheeks shining under the streetlight.

They were listening to Willie Nelson when Lily walked into Erica's rec room after changing her clothes at home. Franklin was swiveling back and forth on a barstool. Daniel was lounging on the sofa, his legs stretched out, boots crossed. She was glad the tempo was slow, that hyperactive Erica hadn't already whipped them into a frenzy. Anything alcoholic would put her out to-night, she was so tired.

"What'll you have in your Tab, Lily?" Erica asked. "No, I'm just kidding. We're drinking hot buttered rum."

"Do you have some Tab?" Lily asked.

"Oh, come on, you wouldn't! Relax a little. I'm only putting a teaspoon of rum in for flavor."

Lily shrugged as she sat down beside Daniel. Erica would do as she pleased anyhow.

"Where you been hanging out?" Daniel asked.

"What do you mean?"

"I mean, 'Where you been hanging out?'"

Lily smiled. "I've been busy."

"Doing what?"

"You know...cheerleader tryouts took most of two weeks. Did Franklin tell you about the new sophomore squad this year?"

"You're changing the subject." He reached for the peanuts on the coffee table and offered her some. She refused.

"You know about last week," Lily said just above a whisper. "I did a little number on the whole neighborhood, I guess."

"I was really worried about you. Everyone was."

She wanted to tell him how stupid she'd been, how sorry she was that he'd got sucked in on it, but the words gave way as her facial tic began. She turned away from him, pressed her lips together.

"Don't worry about it." Daniel gave her a squeeze on the back of the neck. "Hey," he went on, "Rogers over there thinks you're a better cheerleader than anyone who made the varsity. I think you got yourself a fan." They both looked at Franklin, who was carrying on an animated conversation with Erica about business. At the moment he was spouting World War II slogans: "Zip the lip and save a ship!"

Erica laughed.

"Ever hear, 'Shut your traps and beat the Japs'?"

"Imagine calling them 'Japs,'" Erica said, turning thumbs down.

"He's too much," Daniel said quietly.

"Really! In more ways than one!"

Then Erica was handing Lily a mug of steaming, rum-laced cider. Lily breathed in the aroma, remembering she hadn't eaten anything since her lunch of cottage cheese and pear. A sip wouldn't hurt, a swallow now and one a little later.

"The battling bastards of Bataan!" Franklin's voice rose in a war cry.

"Enough of World War II," Erica said as she set down her mug. "We're going to dance."

Erica lifted two records from the rack. "Disco first, for you hot-blooded youths," she said in her deejay voice, "and a golden oldie for you folks in the nursing homes...." She danced away from the stereo and back to the middle of the room, snapping her fingers to the beat. Then Erica reached out a hand for Daniel, pulled him up to be her partner. They moved away, to the tile floor at the opposite end of the game room where the light was considerably dimmer.

Sipping at her drink, Lily watched them, recognizing the knife edge of jealousy which scored her insides. Daniel was beautiful, his movements catlike, sinuous. Unsmiling, Erica followed him. They didn't touch. They didn't need to. The dance was very sexy.

Franklin came over from the bar, forsaking the layout of snacks, and sat next to Lily. "They sure look great together, don't they?"

She nodded, found herself suddenly with a mouthful of peanuts and more in her hand.

"He's one good-looking nigger," he whispered.

Lily drew back. "Don't you *ever* call him that!"

Franklin stared at her. "I don't mean anything by it. It's just... it's just something to say."

Lily stood quickly and walked to the bar. *Ignoramous! Stupid, ignorant fat-ass!* She wondered how he'd like to be called names! She hadn't heard Daniel called "nigger" since grade school. That's where Franklin belonged, back on the playground with the other nasty little boys.

"Sorry," he said, following her, "I got a big mouth sometimes." *Big enough for both feet!*

Lily spread liver sausage on a cracker with quick, jabbing movements. She leaned back against the bar, eating as she watched them dance. Turning to the food again, she dipped a carrot, then celery into the sour cream. She washed it down with the rum drink. Franklin stood watching her, plainly repentant.

"I really made you mad, didn't I?"

She answered by spreading two crackers and handing him one. If she could keep him eating, he wouldn't ask her to dance and she wouldn't have to refuse. *Nigger! What subculture had he come from?*

The ploy worked. The two of them made sizable inroads on the braunschweiger by the time the second record slipped into place.

Now Erica was coming across the room, her hand reaching out for Franklin this time.

"Slow numbers next," Erica said, still breathless. "Hoagy Carmichael." Little bright spots of perspiration dotted her face. "Dance with me, Franklin?"

Daniel sat down beside Lily at the red-bricked bar, waving Erica on. "Thanks. You're a good dancer," he complimented her as she walked off.

"So are you," Lily said to Daniel. "You never danced much at Clarkson, did you?"

"I thought it was sissy, I guess. I was the big jock in high school, remember? Or trying to be." He dipped a corn chip and held it to Lily's mouth. She accepted it. He fixed one for himself.

"It's our turn," Daniel said after they'd sat quietly through "Stardust," watching Erica teach Franklin how to lead. She kept saying, "See? Isn't it easy?" It didn't *look* easy, with the top of Franklin's head tucked under Erica's chin, but neither of them seemed to care.

Lily moved into Daniel's arms. "String of Pearls" spun out its soft, sweet strains, tender as anything. Daniel's hand was warm on her waist. She was so close she could hear him breathe. She couldn't believe this was happening to her! She was in Daniel's arms and it was all right.

The record ended all too soon, of course. Stepping back, smiling, Daniel bowed formally to Lily. He clicked the heels of his boots.

Then he turned and repeated the bow in front of Franklin, who was leaning against the wall watching. "May I have this dance?" Daniel asked.

"Oh, gracious," Franklin squeaked, "if you insist!"

Erica cracked up. She got rid of the forties record in a hurry, put on a tape. They drifted back to the soft chairs and the coffee table.

"Say, I'd better call my dad." Franklin looked at his watch.

"It's okay," Daniel said, "you don't have to dance with me if you don't want to."

Franklin hooted.

Erica showed him the phone but told him he had to have some pizza before he left. "I'll be insulted if you don't stay," she said as she went upstairs to round up more food.

Lily herself ate half a small pizza before they broke up. She could have eaten more, but there were only two. She also drank a can of Coke and helped herself to two cookies when Erica passed them around. She couldn't understand what was happening. It felt as if something had snapped. Something tight, like a straitjacket, had snapped, and *she* came tumbling out.

Someone else was in her skin. The *horrified* Lily stood against the wall, scolding and fretting, warning that she'd be sorry. But the Lily sitting there beside Daniel didn't care.

Tonight it was all right to eat and laugh and flirt. It was okay to touch. Daniel wasn't like Erica's John Hazeltine. He wasn't going to ask her to bed.

Lily leaned against Daniel's shoulder, there where they sat crosslegged at the coffee table. Once her hand rested briefly on his knee.

"Would you share those peanuts?" she asked, smiling right into his eyes, a trick she'd learned from Erica.

Twelve

Lily woke in the middle of the night, the urgency of a full bladder getting her to her feet at once. She staggered to the bathroom and onto the john.

Suddenly awake, the realization of her eating binge at Erica's hit her like a blast of arctic air. Cold crept up through her ankles and knees, producing a shudder that spiraled along her spine. Ninety-three pounds she'd weighed at seven that morning. Now her belly was puffy and full under her hands. She'd ruined it all!

"What have I done?" she whispered over and over, blaming Erica, the rum, Franklin, who had sat there watching her eat with that Jack Sprat look on his face—as if he couldn't imagine where she was putting it all.

Lily strained to get every bit of fluid out of her body, pushing and pressing where she imagined her bladder to be.

The food's digested now. It's part of me! Goose bumps lifted along her arms and legs, signaling cold and panic and remorse.

Suddenly she thought of Ex-Lax. Of course! She had to get rid of the poisons some way. A laxative was perfect! Why hadn't she taken one last night?

Still shivering, Lily tiptoed downstairs to the main bathroom, scolding herself for having fallen asleep so contentedly. It was the full stomach that did it. The weight-loss guidebook warned of the narcotic effects of a big meal.

My God, I broke all the rules, didn't I? Stuffing myself... flirting with Daniel. What must he think of me?

Lily trembled as she pinched off three sections of Ex-Lax. The sweet, dark laxative melted in her mouth and slipped down her throat. One more square, to be sure. Already she felt tremendous relief. The laxative would take care of the gluttony.

As for Daniel, she'd have to stay away from him, that's all. What else could she do? Maybe her mother was right. Maybe she was vulgar and unladylike, bent on disgracing the family. She didn't want to end up being like Erica, she knew that for sure.

Lily crawled back into bed and buried her face in the pillow. Control of her body wasn't enough. She'd have to keep reins on her emotions as well.

Dr. Jessica Coburn answered her phone the next morning at nine-fifty, ten minutes before Lily's appointed Saturday morning hour. She nodded, listening.

"I'm sorry to hear that, Mrs. Jamison. Do you think she could make it later today? I've had a four-o'clock cancellation."

She was assured that Lily was much too ill—a virus, perhaps. No, she didn't have a fever.

"Is diarrhea a recurring problem with her?" Dr. Coburn drew circles on her yellow pad. "It hasn't happened, say, in the past three or four months?"

She listened.

"Mrs. Jamison, when she feels up to it, put her on the bathroom scales, would you? That is, if you don't get too much resistance. Dr. Snyder and I are having a phone conference, and that information would be helpful."

She listened again.

"Yes, by all means, check with him. And thank you for calling. I'll set her up for next Saturday, then, at ten."

After the phone call, Dr. Coburn returned Lily's file to the receptionist, who clucked sympathetically. "Mark it a 'No show,' Dorothy. Their medical reports show nothing wrong, but they look like perambulating skeletons when they get to me. I suspect we have a case of primary anorexia here."

Thirteen

Lily's alarm had buzzed at 5:00 A.M. She'd been at her desk translating Ovid ever since. Already she felt as if she'd put in eighteen hours, though it was still before breakfast. No matter. The C+ on her last Latin test blew her away.

Now Lily stretched out on her unmade bed and closed her eyes. Today there was no way to get out of seeing Dr. Coburn, though she'd successfully avoided her for the past three weeks. Her mother was still mad because she'd had to cancel two appointments in a row, the first due to that sudden and severe diarrhea. The next Saturday she had begged her mother to take her shopping. "Nothing fits!" she'd said, moaning. She knew her mother couldn't resist an all-day shopping trip.

So her personal shopping consultant, Karen Jamison, had escorted her through all five ready-to-wear departments of Dorbach's! As it turned out, seeing Coburn would have been easier.

Lily breathed deeply, listening to the morning sounds from downstairs. Her senses were so acute since she'd lost weight. Sounds were sharper, smells were keen and penetrating, colors were somehow more intense. She herself might feel depressed, but her senses were on a perpetual high.

She heard an egg cracking. Stirring sounds now, the spoon

against the stainless steel bowl. She hoped her mother wasn't making pancakes for *her*. She wasn't up to having a battle today.

Lily ran her hands across her stomach, noting with satisfaction how she sort of caved in there under her nightie. Her hipbones were showing now, for sure. She turned on her side, raised herself on one elbow, then squinted along the sharp angles of her shoulder and hip. She looked exactly like the magazine ads for Chalk Garden Lingerie. Eighty-seven pounds was definitely right for her.

But the pose was too hard to sustain. She rolled to her stomach and collapsed face-down into her pillow. She was so tired! How could she make it through the day?

In two minutes, Lily was up again, dressing, hurrying. She'd had cramps earlier, sitting at her desk. She supposed her period would start now, of all times. Being so much overdue had scared her at first. It was almost as if Snell had hexed her that day in the office, waving her dumb newspaper clipping over Lily like a witch's wand: "So be it, heh, heh, heh!"

Lily buttoned up her blouse, then pulled on a fuzzy sweater. She'd wear the new burgundy blazer, too. Her clothes would add a pound on the scales and give her a bulky look besides.

What a drag! When I get to be my own boss, I won't have to answer to anyone! I'll do exactly as I please!

She yanked up the zipper of her pants and locked the tab in place with a vicious jab.

Coburn's face lit up like a tournament scoreboard when Lily walked into her office at five minutes after ten.

"You made it!" She spread her arms wide. "Sit down...sit!"

From the top of her dark curls to the expressive hands which wouldn't stay put on the desk blotter, Coburn still looked like the newest girl in the steno pool. Today she wore a leather vest and two slender gold chains which showed at the throat of her blouse. Lily approved. It was the "studied careless look" her mother abhorred.

Lily chose the hard chair again, feeling permanently assigned there for some reason.

"One minute," Dr. Coburn got to her feet. "Let's weigh you first today." She handed Lily the clipboard, then directed her toward the supply room that housed the pop and the mice and all the other junk.

Lily stood on the scales. "It looks like...eighty-eight pounds," she said a minute later. Coburn didn't check for herself, just stood there holding two cans of diet drink. *Does she trust me?* Lily waited a decent interval, then stepped off.

Coburn grinned. "Less five ounces for the clipboard."

"Oh, I'm sorry!" Lily felt ridiculous. She hadn't meant to do that!

"Yeah, everybody weighs the clipboard." Coburn breezed on past her.

Lily marked her weight on the chart, then pulled her boots on again. *I know what we'll be talking about today!* She took her seat grim-set for a tug-of-war. *It's my body! She doesn't know what's best for me!*

Coburn arranged her pad and the pencils she never used, took a hearty drink of Tab, then settled back in her comfortable chair.

"For starters today, since it's been so long, why don't you just tell me how you've been."

Lily was caught off guard. She laughed nervously. "I've been fine."

"Good. Terrific, in fact! Then let's begin this way: First, tell me about your high point of the past few weeks. Then I'll ruin everything by asking about your low point. But think it over. Take your time."

Lily knew immediately what her high point was, but did she want to talk about it? Jessica Coburn sat there rocking, sipping at her drink, the picture of endless patience. How could she be so sure *this* patient would cooperate? Lily wiped the moisture off the bottom of the can, stalling.

"There was only one high point," she said at last.

"One's enough."

"Well...some of us got together after the cheerleader initiation. You know...a kind of impromptu thing. Everyone had been out throwing snowballs, and we sort of ended up at Erica's place down the street."

"What happened? What made that so special?"

Lily shifted on the chair. "Oh, it was fun. We relaxed."

"And you don't do that very often, right?"

"No. I mean yes, you're right."

"All the cheerleaders were there?"

"Oh, no, it was just friends from my end of the street, plus Fat Franklin, who is a cheerleader. Four of us."

"Fat Franklin." Dr. Coburn chuckled. "Who was the other couple?"

"We weren't there as couples!" *She and Franklin? No way! What made her think that?*

"Sorry, you're all neighbor friends, I get it. Have you known these kids very long?"

"Daniel, since I was six. That's when he moved in next door." Lily wrinkled her nose thinking about the Walker-Nelsons. "Erica's lived there forever. Franklin's new at our school. He's on the sophomore squad."

"So he has a weight problem? Do you find his appearance offensive?"

"Really."

"I'm still wondering why the party was your high point. You beat everyone at video games?"

"No, we danced mostly...and talked."

"You danced with Daniel?"

Lily dug her fingernails into her palm. "Yes."

"I take it he's someone special."

Don't answer.

"Have you and Daniel ever dated?"

"No." Her face had gone red, she could feel it.

Lily took a long sip of Tab, concentrated on staring into the can afterward. Coburn herself paused, made some notes, then rolled her chair closer to the desk.

"Okay...now, let's talk about your low point," she said, looking at Lily from behind her big Orphan Annie glasses. "Had any low points lately?"

Lily was relieved. She could spend the rest of the hour talking about her low point: the shopping trip with her mother. To begin with, they had to buy everything at Dorbach's because her mother did so many ads for them. That in itself was frustrating. Then to have her mother insist on high-fashion lines when *she* wanted jeans and sportswear...

But her psychiatrist wasn't so much interested in how their tastes differed as in how Lily handled their arguments. She usually gave in, that's what. So she looked like a Dorbach's ad at school every day! So what?

"How do you feel about compromising so much?" Dr. Coburn asked. Then, finally, "Do you ever shop alone or with a friend?"

"I never have," Lily admitted. "Besides, it's my mother's *thing*. She's always had the last word on what I wear. She knows what's 'voguey.' I'm not sure I could pick out"—Lily searched for the best way to say it—"what looks good on me. She has a hard enough time!" Lily laughed nervously. "She used to say I was 'plump.' Now she says I'm too bony. I can't please her."

"Would she be hurt if you went alone?"

"She'd die, that's all."

"What was the reason for this shopping trip?" Coburn drew polka dot bows on her yellow pad. "You know, was it your birthday or something?"

"No, my clothes just didn't fit very well."

"Yeah, that's a good reason. What size did you wear before you lost weight?"

Lily considered lying, but remembered in time that Dr. Snyder, Coburn's accomplice, had her weight down in black and white from the day she was born.

"I wore nines and tens a year ago."

"And now you're into—"

"Fives." Lily couldn't keep the pride out of her voice.

Coburn's fingertips met in front of her chin, forming a steeple. "That's a big change. Was it a year ago, then, when you decided to get serious about your weight?"

"Last spring. When the scales hit a hundred twenty-nine, I guess I got scared. I started dieting and running after basketball season was over in March."

Coburn lifted the clipboard off the corner of her desk and studied it. "In eight months you've lost forty-two pounds. Maybe more if we subtract the extra weight of those winter clothes." She gave Lily a direct, no-nonsense look. "What would the ideal weight be for someone your height?"

Coburn left her chair then, walked to the windows beside Lily, and began to adjust the blinds. Lily blinked. The sun, which had made patterns on the floor like so many dinosaur ribs, now flooded the room with light. She loved the warmth, but the sunlight was so bright it hurt her eyes.

Dr. Coburn lifted Lily's wrist, examined it. "Medium bone structure, I'd say. What do you think? How much should you weigh—ideally?"

"I like my present weight. I wouldn't want to be any heavier than I am."

Coburn nodded, looking down at Lily. "Are you still running regularly?"

"Yes. Five or six days a week."

"How far?"

Lily shrugged. "I got up to five miles, but now I'm doing about two."

"Doesn't running increase your appetite? Running makes me absolutely ravenous!"

"I don't notice it. Once I decided not to be hungry, I wasn't hungry. Sometimes I crave something, that's all."

Coburn curled up in the hibiscus chair opposite Lily, then slipped off her heels and tucked her feet under her skirt.

"When did your periods stop, by the way?"

First Snell, now Coburn!

"At this weight," Coburn went on, sounding matter-of-fact, "you'd have experienced amenorrhea. That's a big word which means you've stopped menstruating. I assume that's already happened."

"I haven't had a period for a while, but I didn't think it was anything to worry about."

"I'm going to tell you some things about yourself. Afterward, you tell me if I'm right, okay? Would you do that?"

Coburn sat up straight. She pretended to hold something round and solid in her hands. She smoothed its surface in pantomime.

"This is a crystal ball...and I'm Madame Fifi. In this all-knowing orb I shall read your present. Not your past or your future, but your present."

Coburn really got into it, peering into the imaginary ball, wiping it off with her sleeve for a better look.

"Ah, yes, it's coming clear now. There she is, a pretty blond girl. She's reading Emily Dickinson and wearing a burgundy blazer." She looked up quizzically. "Anyone we know?"

Lily smiled faintly.

"Now I see her running, but I can tell by her face that it's a great effort. She wants to stop in the worst way...to slow down and rest...but she won't let herself. She must keep on and on,

[105]

until she finishes the course. Her legs ache and her chest hurts, but her iron will prevails. The body must be subjugated to the mind, totally!"

"Oops, scene changes." She threw Lily a look of apology. "Dumb ball, no transitions," she muttered.

This time Lily laughed.

"Now she's sitting at a school desk. The room is drafty and she's cold. She's always cold lately. 'Turn up the sun!' she says and wishes she could. The lesson's dull, wouldn't you know? The plastic seat is hard . . . she starts thinking about lunch . . . her stomach growls. She wishes she could eat, but food has become a poison to her. Maybe she'll make a cake at home tonight. Yeah, she'll bake a cake! She thinks about her father and how much he likes a homemade cake and how he'll eat it and praise her for baking it.

"But alas! She must bring herself back to the classroom to concentrate on the lecture. A low grade would spoil her perfect record. Who wants to be second best after always being best? She grits her teeth and listens, though she'd rather be curled up in some sunny corner like a sleeping cat.

"Hey"—Coburn leaned forward, holding the ball out for Lily to see—"look! She turned herself into a cat. Why would she do that?"

Lily pulled away. "I'm not exactly into crystal balls."

"You were in mine. Then you disappeared."

"Oh, well"—shrugging—"I'm always disappearing."

Coburn threw back her head and laughed. She ended the dramatics by setting the ball squarely in Lily's lap. "Did you see yourself there at all?"

"Yes. But my dad likes pecan pies, not cakes. He does say no one makes them better than I do."

"You see? Madame Fifi sees true! She may get her pies mixed up with her cakes, but she sees true."

Madame stood and walked back to her desk. "Now you know. I like to play games. Can't help myself. However—" her voice grew serious as she turned back to face Lily—"anorexia nervosa is no game, though some people end up playing it for keeps."

Anorexia? Lily mouthed the word, experiencing a wave of *déjà vu* that returned her to Snell's office.

"What's that?" Lily asked, pretending ignorance.

"It's an illness. It can—in fact, it already has—affected your health."

"My health?" Lily squeaked. For the first time, she wanted Coburn to go on talking, though she knew their hour was nearly up. "If I do have *that*, how did I get it? I mean, how can someone get it without knowing? I'm not sick, you know. Dr. Snyder himself says I'm not."

"You developed it as you lost weight and began starving your body."

"I told you I'm never hungry. How could I be starving?"

"At eighty-seven pounds, you're *under*nourished. Your output, your physical activity, exceeds your intake, and has for some time now. The starvation itself produces some strange disturbances. For one thing, the brain gets confused signals. The body may be screaming, 'Feed me! Feed me!' but the brain has taken its phone off the hook and doesn't get the message."

Lily shivered. The room was suddenly cold, though the sunlight was still streaming in.

"I know you have a lot of questions, Lily, everyone does..." Dr. Coburn reached into a drawer. "I have a pamphlet here which I've prepared especially for persons with anorexia. I want you and your parents to read it.

"Now, I know you'll love having yet another assignment," she went on, "but I'd like all three of you to write a letter to me this week. Separately, please. No fair comparing notes. Just stick them in the mail before Wednesday or Thursday. I want each of you to tell me why you think you developed anorexia nervosa."

Coburn's last words, after the telephone buzzed for the next patient, were, "Hold onto those eighty-seven pounds now!"

In the reception room a teenager waited, reading a magazine. She hung over the chair on both sides, a sloppy fat sideshow freak. *I'd die if I looked like that,* Lily thought. Then she remembered the little metal plate on Coburn's scales—"Capacity, 300 pounds"—and she started to giggle. Down fourteen stairs and out onto the sidewalk, she laughed until her cheeks were wet. Her mother would think she'd been crying!

Fourteen

Dear Dr. Coburn:

Howard and I were married seven years before I became pregnant with Lily. When she was born, I was thirty years old. I gave up all my free-lance illustrating and devoted myself to raising our dream child. We rarely used a baby-sitter and never took trips without her. She was content to be with us, an extremely easy child to raise, and we were just as content being parents. We never expected to have another child, so we occupied ourselves educating and entertaining Lily.

Our daughter was nearly twelve when I found myself pregnant with her sister, June. The news was a shock to Lily, who had been the center of our lives so long, though Howard and I were secretly delighted. Of course, we never let Lily know that. We could tell she was less than thrilled. I had several talks with her at the time, but she was very uncomfortable when I tried to explain the "facts of life."

Lily actually became physically ill the five days I was in the hospital. Howard had his hands full, too, with a business crisis, so we remember Juju's birth as a harrowing time.

I'm explaining Lily's background in detail because I believe her psychological problems began when her sister was born.

Though she was always bright, Lily now began working furiously at school to make the best grades. At home she became a perfectionist, doing every task as thoroughly as I would myself. She put in long hours at the Racquet Club with her father, improving her tennis. Naturally we praised her, realizing that she was competing with Juju the whole time. In gymnastics, she took the top ribbons. She was captain of the cheerleaders, too, last year. She had to be the best in whatever she did.

Last spring she undertook dieting in the same headlong fashion. She'd been slightly overweight, even with all her activities, so I was glad to see Lily undertake a serious diet. I bought her books on nutrition, a calorie guide, and agreed to fix low-calorie meals. The first week she gained half a pound and ended up blaming me. Then when she started running, she began to lose weight.

If Lily has anorexia nervosa as described in the pamphlet, it may be a thing she's doing to spite us. I think she's trying to get her father's attention by making a spectacle of herself. Howard plays tennis with his business associates now that Lily prefers running, but even though he has little time for her, she's still quick to side with him. She offers nothing to me these days but her dirty laundry!

Juju, of course, is the one Howard finds amusing right now. She's so different from Lily we're amazed they could be sisters. Juju's the one with a mind of her own, who's always pushing our rules to the limits.

I am starting to be worried about Lily's appearance. I didn't realize how pathetically thin she was until a recent shopping trip. Whatever suggestions you have, we'll be glad to follow through. We've cherished our girls and our harmonious and happy life together. We can't let Lily's wilfulness destroy all we've worked so hard to accomplish.

Thank you for the opportunity to express myself in this letter.
I hope we'll be meeting you soon.

Very sincerely yours,
Karen Jamison

Dear Dr. Coburn,

If I have anorexia nervosa, as you explain it in the booklet,
then I guess I enjoy having it. I love being in control of my own
body. I love choosing what I eat and how much of it and I don't
want to give it up.

I've always tried not to disappoint my parents or my teachers
and I hope I'm not disappointing you (I know this isn't what you
want me to say), but the dieting is something I do for me. Being
thin and in condition is important to *me*!!!

Furthermore, I've discovered I don't need to eat much. I can
get by on less than I ever dreamed and still feel full. I feel sorry
for my friends who haven't experienced the same power over
themselves. Their brains are fuzzy with Fritos and Cokes and all
that cafeteria garbage they call lunch.

I'd feel like a complete nonperson if I couldn't control my own
appetite. Now that my weight is in the eighties, I feel light, filled
with light, too, and pure. Sometimes I imagine I can see through
my skin and past the veins, inside to the real me. The shadow I
cast is only my X ray.

Lily

Dr. Coburn:

My wife will probably come up with some deep, dark psychological reason for Lily being the way she is. I'm a plainer-
spoken person than my wife is, so I may be more blunt. Here's
my opinion.

I think Lily is trying to be like her mother, who's been on a diet from the first day I knew her. Lily copies her in other ways, too. She used to bring her artwork home from school to show us, but her mother could never look at Lily's drawings without making a suggestion. Sometimes she'd take the gum eraser and change something to suit herself. This year Lily didn't sign up for art, though her mother had a fit when she found out. I think Lily was just plain discouraged. She knew she'd never be as good as Karen.

Also, Lily's had too much. She's spoiled. I can't believe she'd have quit eating if food were scarce in our house. The fridge is always full. Karen makes a triple-decker cake, then throws half of it out uneaten. (My wife's a terrific cook, but she has the appetite of a bird herself and generally misjudges how much we can eat.) Having grown up in a household where meat was for Sundays and the girls got new dresses only at Easter and Christmas, I have a hard time understanding Lily and even her mother. They don't appreciate what they have. I hope you can help her, though I admit to having doubts.

Getting her to eat is our main concern and the thing you should work on. She's the apple of my eye, Dr. Coburn. It hurts me to see her going downhill.

Lily's father,
Howard Jamison

Fifteen

Daniel sat studying the menu in the Taco Time. Across from him, her chin scarcely higher than the napkin holder, sat Grandma Perry, her lips stitched together as she weighed the merits of soft shells over hard ones.

"Got to have somethin' kind of mushy," she reminded Daniel. "This old mouth ain't what she used to be."

Daniel ended up ordering two burritos for his grandmother and three tacos for himself. He bought an extra-large drink for her, too, which turned out to be a twelve-ounce error in judgment. Each time she wanted a sip she had to lower the root beer into her lap to get to the straw.

"Got more root beer than brains," she said and grinned, hunching up her shoulders.

Daniel chuckled. Grandma Perry could always make him laugh, no matter how bad he felt.

"What's eatin' you, Daniel? This is my Saturday outin'. If we got to take your troubles to lunch, you'd better introduce 'em."

"I'm okay, honest."

Grandma Perry sat back to make way for their baskets when they arrived, smiling happily at the girl who brought them.

"No, you ain't!" she whispered the minute they were alone. "You've been botherin' about somethin' all day."

Daniel poured extra-hot sauce on his taco. "You tell me, Grandma. You're the one with the sixth sense." She could never locate her glasses, but she could smell "trouble" like any blood-hound.

Grandma Perry turned a burrito from one end to the other, studying its possibilities. For a minute Daniel thought she'd lost out on the conversation, she seemed so absorbed in the neat tortilla wrapping. But she hadn't lost her place.

"You worry about school too much, studyin' every night until the wee hours. I think Daniel's forgotten all about havin' fun."

"Grandma!" he scolded. "I'm having fun right now."

"Oh, shush now, you should have a girlfriend, nice young man like you."

"Naw, I have to make decent grades."

"Don't you like girls?"

"Sure I do. I always have a good time with Lily and Erica."

"White girls!" Grandma spat out the words.

"So?" He hoped his grandmother wouldn't get started on *that*.

"Haven't you met any nice black girls up to that university?" Grandma Perry clamped down on a bean burrito.

Daniel grinned. It was uncanny the way she could sniff out the truth. Short on memory, she was long—even scary—on insight. "How'd you guess?" he asked.

Her eyes sparkled. "What's her name?"

"Kimberly. She's a sister to this guy in my computer science class. Blake wants me to take her out."

Grandma Perry rolled her eyes heavenward, offering thanks to her Calvary Baptist Jesus, no doubt.

"But Kimberly's only half the problem." Daniel doctored up another taco. "Lily's the other half."

"I'm very fond of that girl, same as you, but don't you be mixin' up—"

"Grandma, I promised Lily I'd come over to the Jamisons' tonight. They're having Mom and Dad for cocktails. For some reason, they kind of casually included me for their Christmas open house."

"One on each arm." His grandma cackled. "Uuuh, unh!"

Daniel smiled across the table at his wizened little grandmother, whose worries had just been put to rest. She could concentrate on her weekend outing now. As far as she was concerned, the prospect of Daniel's meeting a nice black girl settled absolutely everything.

For Daniel, having two social obligations on the same night, though improbable, was not impossible. He'd work it out somehow. What bothered him most was how his grades stood this quarter. Finals were coming up in a week. He'd lined up one tutor for physics and another for calculus without telling his folks about either. If he couldn't make it in computer science...
then what?

"That's where it's at, son," his dad kept telling him.

"Good jobs, good pay, a real future" was his mother's line. "Everybody's looking for educated blacks right now."

Daniel poked the lettuce back into his taco. He couldn't fail, that's all. He hadn't been programmed for it.

That evening at the Jamisons', Lily walked into her mother's room wearing her new dress. She turned sideways in front of the full-length mirror, appraising the chiffon dress from another angle.

"Do you like it?" she asked.

"Love it! See how flattering the drape is there over the bosom? That dress has marvelous lines, Lily."

Naturally her mother would think so. She'd picked it out.

"I like this creamy color," Lily said, trying to be agreeable, though she worried that she might be overdressed. Would Daniel think she was putting on? If he wore a suit tonight, she'd feel all right in a dressy dress. But what if he came in slacks and a sweater?

Lily began to unzip, then turned to let her mother finish.

"Daniel and I aren't staying here for the whole evening, you know. We'll probably go to the Sports Mall."

"Are you sure he'll want to go? That means changing clothes and everything."

"Mother," Lily said impatiently, "I know Daniel. He hates stuffy affairs. We'll run a little on the indoor track...play some racquetball or something. So don't make a big thing of it when we excuse ourselves. Okay?"

Karen Jamison sighed as she replaced Lily's dress on the hanger and laid it on the bed. She was in a robe and slippers herself, about to get dressed. Lily noticed how old she looked without her makeup. She'd hate being that old when the time came, she knew she would.

"Lily," her mother said, frowning, "turn around. Look at yourself."

Lily did as she was told, tilting her head to one side. "My slip's too big, isn't it?" She gathered the extra fabric of the slip in her hand and pulled it tight at the waistline.

"I mean *you*, not the slip."

"I look okay. What's wrong?"

Her mother ran a finger down Lily's backbone. "You look skeletal, *emaciated*. Can't you see that?"

Lily stared at her mother in the mirror. *Maybe I should point out a few of your new wrinkles.*

"Even your hair has lost its luster."

Lily pulled away from her mother's touch. "Will you leave me alone? I look all right."

"You look like you've just come out of a concentration camp, that's all. Don't you know how worried your father and I are about you? We love you!" Karen turned away, shaking her head. "I don't think that psychiatrist is doing you one bit of good. You've seen her four times and you're still losing weight. You complain about constipation and stomach aches, and is it any wonder?"

"See you later," Lily said, walking out on her mother. She snatched up her dress on the way. Lecture 39B could take a whole hour and she still had to shower.

Later, blow-drying her hair, Lily thought back to her morning session with Dr. Coburn. They'd spent a lot of time talking about how the human body uses food, how it begins to live on itself when starvation occurs. It was all very gruesome. Lily thought at first her therapist was just trying to scare her, especially when she hauled out this picture of a girl who couldn't even hold up her head because the neck muscles had deteriorated so.

"Imogene," Dr. Coburn called her, sounding sad when she said her name. Imogene had died. But she'd weighed only sixty-four pounds. Lily wasn't going to diet down to sixty-four pounds. No way!

Then Coburn and she worked out daily menus of food Lily liked, and she promised to stick to it or make appropriate substitutions. "Nibble a lot," Coburn had said. "It's easier that way."

Tonight she'd nibble. She had skipped lunch so she could. Also, her mother would go into total depression if she didn't show some evidence of eating. Drinking was something else. "Only one drink," her mother told Lily earlier, "and have some snacks with it. Daniel can have more than one if he likes. He's of age, of course."

Tell me about it! Lily turned off the hair dryer and plugged in the curling brush. She was so sick of the interminable instructions. She herself couldn't wait to be "of age." She'd leave home as soon as she could...or would she? Deep down, the idea scared her. Terrified her, in fact. Maybe she'd never be able to break away, make it on her own. Maybe she was tied forever to her incredible mother. Drawn irresistibly to the dazzling light of freedom, she might end up like the summer moths that sizzled in the electric exterminator. Lily frowned. How could she be so morbid when she was going to see Daniel tonight?

A short while later, twirling in front of her mirror, touching the soft folds of her dress, she was glad to be sliver-thin. She really was striking! She touched perfume to her ears and wrists, blew herself a kiss of approval.

Daniel would probably know she was trying to impress him. He wasn't a bit formal...not Daniel. But, then, it was her own fault. She'd let her mother talk her into this dress.

When the door chimes sounded, Lily knew Daniel and his parents had arrived. They were always the first. She was glad, though her mother had done a lot of rushing around at the last minute, muttering, "Why can't the Perrys be fashionably late like everyone else?"

"Come in, come in!" She heard her mother warbling at the door, the perfect hostess now. "Merry Christmas, Florence, Paul."

Her dad's voice next: "Glad you could join us this year, Daniel."

Lily started down the curved stairway, smiling at the Perrys below. Good, Daniel was in a suit. They'd look perfect together.

Then she saw that Daniel wasn't alone. Standing beside him was a tall, gorgeous black girl. Lily froze.

Daniel was introducing her, smiling and nodding, looking very proud.

"Mrs. Jamison, I'd like you to meet Kimberly Reems. And this is Mr. Jamison."

"Do call us Howard and Karen." Lily's mother took Kimberly's hand. "I'm very happy to meet you."

"They can't stay," Florence Perry explained. "They're on their way out, but Daniel wanted to come by." Then Florence caught sight of Lily. "Oh, my! Look how lovely *you* are!"

Lily took a deep breath and continued to the bottom of the stairs, where she was hugged by Florence, then kissed on the top of the head by Paul, who carried his own sprig of mistletoe. Lily laughed, but it came out sounding hollow.

"Lily, this is Kim Reems," Daniel said.

She could feel her mother's eyes on her, Daniel's eyes, Kimberly's liquid brown eyes.

"Hi," Lily said, smiling big and false.

"We can't stay very long." Daniel was falling all over himself making excuses. "But I wanted to say Merry Christmas. We have to meet her brother and his date in about twenty minutes."

"That's nice," Lily said.

It was Juju who saved her, who came thumping down the stairs in her Mickey Mouse pajamas calling out, "I wanta see Daniel!"

Everyone laughed. Juju's crush on Daniel was a joke in both families. In seconds she was in his arms, her legs wrapped around his middle, hugging him with a death grip.

"Juju, he's all dressed up!" Karen scolded.

Daniel grinned. "It's okay. This one's going to be a first-class tackle someday."

Kimberly laughed, her white teeth blinding Lily. She tickled Juju's foot. "How old are you, Mickey Mouse?"

"Not old enough for cocktail parties," Karen said as she disengaged her younger from Daniel. "Come on, now. Lily will take you back upstairs. Say good night to our guests."

Juju sulked, reluctantly letting Lily take her hand. "I need something to drink. I'm thirsty."

"So is everyone else," Howard said, raising his eyebrows. "Come on in to the bar, folks, and I'll take your orders. There's punch, too."

Then Lily's father had his arm around Kimberly, steering her toward the dining room. "Are you a university student, Kim?..." His voice blended with the Perry's and his wife's. Karen herself had taken possession of Daniel, chattering away. The door chimes sounded again. Lily retreated up the stairs, squeezing Juju's hand so hard her little sister cried out.

"I don't like you!" Juju pulled away.

"I don't like me either," Lily said.

Juju ran on ahead to her room, slamming the door behind her, yelling threats. She *hated* being excluded from parties.

So do I, Lily thought as she walked toward her own room. *But I won't make a disturbance. Oh, no! I'll just curl up and die. Discreetly.*

Lily closed her bedroom door behind her and unzipped the new party dress, alone now except for the company of her poet.

"Not with a club, the heart is broken...Nor with a stone...A whip so small you could not see it...I've known..."

The dress made a soft rustling around her legs as it fell to the floor. She wondered if Dr. Coburn would sound as sad talking about her as she did about Imogene.

Sixteen

She could see the words printed on a Franklin Rogers lapel pin: "Due to lack of interest . . . Lily Jamison has been canceled."

As far as she was concerned, that was exactly what happened at the Christmas party. She had been stamped "void," and Daniel had done the stamping. She knew it was going to hurt a long, long time. Now, more than ever, staying thin took over as the solitary focus of her life. There was nothing else worth caring about.

At school she carefully avoided her friends, concentrating on the minutest aspects of her schoolwork. At home she stoically kept to her room. With Christmas approaching, it would be so easy to lose control, surrounded as she was by the good smells of her mother's holiday baking.

During this time Lily spent her after-school hours running at the Sports Mall track until she was ready to drop. After returning home she'd throw herself across the bed, falling into a shallow, troubled sleep that made sleeping at night impossible.

Some mornings, dozing at last, she slept right through her alarm. On those days her mother would drive her to school. Once in the car, she'd spill her anxiety all over Lily. "Do you *want* to go to the hospital? Is that what you want? You're just asking to be fed through a tube, you know. I can't believe anyone in her right mind would choose that route over..." On and on. Torrents of words. Lily didn't know what "right mind" meant anymore. Was anybody ever in her right mind? Maybe she'd retreated to her left mind, an amusing idea. Maybe she'd simply left her troublesome mind in order to perfect her body. They couldn't invade her very Self, all those meddlesome adults making the rules. By the time they'd arrive at school her mother would have gone silent again. Mercifully.

Every night when her father came home the arguments flared. Accusations were followed by long, chilly silences. Always they fought about "Lily's condition." Mealtimes, of course, were a farce. She could see her parents counting every forkful of food she took, keeping score, so they could compare afterward. Even Juju didn't divert them now from fighting over Lily. So long as Juju ate, they let her do as she pleased.

Sometimes Lily thought Juju was the only normal person in the family. "I don't care if you don't eat nothing," she'd said to Lily one day, in her own way trying to comfort her sister. A little later, though, she'd walked in on Lily while she was dressing. She'd stared at first, the way she looked at strangers sometimes. Then her face puckered into a question: "Skipper wants to know when you're going to die.... When are you?"

"Get out!" Lily had yelled, charging after her. "Get out of here this minute!"

Suddenly Coburn herself was talking about hospitalization and forced feeding. Lily supposed that was coming next, but none of it seemed real or threatening. Lily had reduced her life to a single concern. One at a time, she had successfully tuned out all other distracting elements.

Daniel had called her once. "Do you want to see a movie on running at the student union?" he'd asked. No, she didn't care to.

Franklin Rogers had invited her to a Christmas party at his

house. They were going roller skating first. "No, I'm not still mad at you. It's just...I've made other plans."

Even Erica had called, asking her to go Christmas shopping.

Untouchable, unreachable, by her own will she had finally achieved a pure and holy state: perfect self-control.

After Christmas, Dr. Coburn sent Lily back to Dr. Snyder for another medical exam and a reevaluation. "She's a very sick girl," Dr. Snyder told her mother in her presence. He had talked about her constipation, her insomnia, her depression...the changes in blood pressure and body temperature...her weight, which had dropped to seventy-eight pounds.

"She's seriously dehydrated," he said. Lily didn't care. It was as if he were talking about someone else.

In the car going home her mother cried, blaming Lily for "bringing them to their knees." Lily hadn't been moved by her mother's tears one way or another.

Throughout the crisis that was building around her, she did worry about one thing: She knew she was hurting her father. But for the first time in ages he was putting his arms around her, calling her his little girl once again. He'd taken to coming in at night to tuck her in, sometimes bringing her a drink of water. He was losing weight, too, she noticed. His belt had been taken up a notch.

"I love you, Daddy," she said one night as he was leaving her room. He was back at her bed in two strides, lifting her in his arms, holding her against him. He was crying. His tears wet her cheek, her neck.

"Oh, Daddy," she apologized, half crying herself, "I'm so sorry. Please don't cry."

He'd held her a long time, rocking her like a baby right there on the side of her bed. Sleep that night was the soundest and sweetest she'd had in weeks.

Finally, as everyone had been predicting, the day arrived. It was the morning after Dr. Snyder's exam. Jessica Coburn called early, telling Mrs. Jamison that Dr. Snyder had made arrangements at the university hospital. Lily was to be admitted around noon and both doctors would see her the same evening. She was to be in a private room, and the parents were asked not to visit or call.

Lily knew what was happening from the snatches of conversation she overheard, but she remained upstairs in bed until her mother came up to pack a bag as she'd been instructed.

"I want to take my patchwork pillow," was all Lily said when her mother appeared in the doorway. Her voice sounded small, like a ten-year-old's, even to her.

Seventeen

"What a beautiful pillow!" the nurse said cheerfully. "This room could stand a little brightening up." She turned Lily around to fasten the back of her hospital gown.

"How about some sunlight?" Lily's mother stepped to the window and adjusted the drapes as if she were in her own living room.

"That's too much," Lily complained.

"I'm sorry, darling. How's that?"

"The old sun gets harsh this time of day," the nurse said, pulling down the bedding.

"I'm cold." Lily knew she was whining, but she couldn't help it. She *was* cold. And scared. She'd never been in a hospital before.

"Would you bring her robe and slippers from the locker, Mrs. Jamison?"

Lily watched the nurse as she bent to pull a footstool out from under the bed. She was overweight like everyone else, her uniform straining across her hips, but she moved fast. She moved so fast Lily hadn't been able to read her nameplate yet.

She held the velour robe for Lily. "Hop on up, now. Dr. Snyder says bed rest. No TV, at least for the time being."

Mrs. Jamison gave Lily a consoling look. "Good thing you brought your school books."

"No books. No knitting or crossword puzzles. We don't even want you to think! Just rest."

P. McPherson. That was her name. Lily looked from the name to the face. McPherson was plain, with freckles and short brown hair. Middle-aged, like her mother.

"Be back in five," she said, winking at Lily. "And you just remember. Your folks can visit you every day as soon as you're better." She nodded at Mrs. Jamison on the way out.

Lily turned away. She knew her mother had to leave and that now was the time. She didn't want to see the hurt look replace her mother's public mask; she didn't want to hear again how much she'd injured them. She knew that song by heart.

"You're going to be all right, Lily," her mother said, patting her hand. "We'll miss you terribly at home, you know that."

Lily clenched her teeth, concentrating on the bedside tray, the pink plastic pitcher sitting in a matching plastic pan. For once, her mother wasn't blaming her.

Then Lily felt cold lips brush her cheek. Quickly, she grabbed her mother around the neck, burying her face in her mother's hair. There were no tears to hold back. They'd dried up like the rest of her body, but she bit her lip until she tasted blood.

They clung to one another without saying a word, as if storing up strength for a long separation. Finally, Karen Jamison pulled away. She picked up her purse and coat and walked quickly to the door.

"Tell Daddy..."

Her mother nodded, but she didn't look back. Lily knew she was crying.

Lily lay there, straining to hear her mother's footsteps. Finally, the nurse came back to the room. This time she carried a small tray with a paper cup on it. She was even more cheerful now that she had her patient all to herself. She began talking at once.

"Lily Jamison is a very nice name. I like the sound of it. Can you imagine going through life as Mary Margaret McPherson?" She slipped a thermometer under Lily's tongue. "I think my mother had it in for me. So I call myself Peggy."

She opened Lily's "comfort kit," setting the lotion, the Kleenex, the bedpan on a shelf under the bedside table. Lily watched, her own icy hands tucked under her arms. Her feet embraced under the sheet, trying to find warmth in one another. Suddenly she couldn't stop shivering.

"Are you still cold?"

Lily nodded.

The nurse left and returned with another blanket. "This one's been heated," she said, tucking it in against Lily's back. "You'll love it."

She read Lily's temperature, marked it on a chart, ejected the disposable tip. Then she took her blood pressure and wrote that down.

"I brought you some Profile. It's something like instant breakfast. If you drink this, you won't have to order a tray tonight. Unless you want to, of course."

The blanket felt so good, the heat penetrating right into her skin, that it was hard to focus on the nurse or what she was talking about.

She held the straw to Lily's lips. "Chocolate fudge," she said, smiling. "Tastes like your basic Saturday night malt at the A&W."

Lily took a sip. She closed her eyes, but the straw stayed there, stuck to her upper lip.

"A couple more swallows, Lily. Did the doctor tell you you're dehydrated? Taking fluids will keep you from being *really* sick."

[127]

"I don't want it." Lily pushed the straw away with her tongue.

"All right. We'll wait awhile."

The nurse walked into the adjoining bathroom, returning with a towel over her shoulder and a pan of water in her hands. She dipped the washcloth, lathered it, then took Lily's hand and began to wash her. Gently, slowly, she massaged each finger. The hot water felt so good. The nurse took a long time with each hand, soaping and washing and rinsing. Then she sponged Lily's face. The warm water was making her very drowsy.

The nurse set the pan aside, placed Lily's hands back under the covers. "Let's try some more of this," she said, her voice calm, friendly. "If you can drink half, I'll wash your feet, too. Hot water's just the ticket for warming up cold feet."

Lily took another sip. It was too sweet.

"You're doing fine," the nurse said, stroking Lily's hair. "Just a little more." She raised Lily's head so she could drink. Their faces were close. "You're terrific, Lily, you really are."

Forcing herself, Lily sucked at the straw. Finally, feeling horribly full, repulsed by the smell and the taste both, she slumped back onto the pillow. She couldn't take another swallow, not even in exchange for warm feet. She pushed the drink away.

P. McPherson didn't comment. She set the paper cup back on the tray and busily went about emptying the wash pan. Even before she left the room, Lily felt herself falling asleep.

Lily awoke hearing voices. It was dark. Was it night now, or had the drapes been pulled? She was too tired to do more than open and close her eyes, but in that second she saw two silhouettes in her doorway. One was Dr. Coburn. She opened her eyes again. Dr. Snyder. They were the ones talking. Two doctors for one patient. Was she that sick?

A third person joined the two at the door. The figures walked into the room. Lily saw Dr. Snyder lift her chart from the rack, then heard the click of the light switch.

"You have company." It was the same nurse, McPherson, standing there beside her. "Did you have a good nap?"

Lily stirred, then sat up, blinking. She raised a hand to shield her eyes from the light.

"Hello, Lily," Dr. Coburn said, moving closer.

Lily lay back. "How long do I have to stay here?"

"Mostly that's up to you."

"In that case, I want to go home tomorrow," Lily said. They might as well know how she felt.

Dr. Snyder found Lily's foot and captured it, right through the blankets and sheet. He was still her bald, red-faced family doctor, but he didn't look right without his white coat.

"I'm going to explain why you're here and I want you to listen very carefully, Lily." He squeezed her toes. "You're severely dehydrated. You haven't been getting enough fluids in your body. When this happens, the electrolyte balance of your blood is upset and your potassium level goes haywire. Not eating and not drinking gets very dangerous at this point. Dr. Coburn and I feel you need some round-the-clock care."

"Couldn't I just stay in bed at home?"

"Afraid not." He shook his head, finally letting go of her foot. "I've ordered an intravenous solution for you. Electrolytes and glucose. You can't get that at home. Don't worry, now, young lady, we'll stay here and see that you get started on the IV. You're going to be A-okay!"

Lily turned her face to the wall. She'd heard enough. If they couldn't poke it down her, they'd stick it in her veins. Two of them, ganging up on her. Just like at home, only here she was more helpless than ever!"

They were talking together now, in low voices, walking toward the door. Then Dr. Snyder left the room. She'd like to stick an IV in him and see how he liked it!

Dr. Coburn came back across the room, dragging a chair from its place against the wall, making rasping sounds that hurt Lily's ears. Coburn unbuttoned her sweater jacket, smiled at her patient.

Roll up your sleeves while you're at it. It's your turn to work me over.

Coburn crossed her legs, made herself comfortable in the visitor's chair.

"I get too nervous to stay in bed," Lily complained, turning to face her psychiatrist. "Can't I get up and walk around?"

"As soon as you've gained a pound, you'll be allowed trips to the bathroom by yourself. That's step one."

"You mean I can't even go to the john?"

"Not yet. You'll have to use the bedpan for the time being."

Lily let out her breath in an angry rush. *IV's and bedpans! You're making me sick!*

"You'll be drinking A&W's—that's what the staff calls them—several times a day until you want solid food. Profile comes in four flavors and it's not bad. I drink it myself when I can't stop for a regular meal."

Lily moaned. The one she'd tasted was awful!

"If you simply can't take nourishment by mouth, Lily, you'll be tube-fed through the nose. That isn't very comfortable. One way or another, we have to prevent further starvation, and it's easier on you if you try to cooperate."

Dr. Coburn leaned toward Lily, resting her arms on the edge of the bed. "You need to drink as much as you can. There's plenty of ice water. Mrs. McPherson will bring you soda pop, Popsicles, bouillon, Jell-O, whatever strikes your fancy. In fact, she's bringing all of us some fruit juice right now."

Lily made a face. Why didn't they just stick the hose in her

nose and get it over with? Blimplike, she'd expand and expand
.... They'd like that!

Coburn must have read her look because she reached out and
squeezed her hand.

"I know you don't want to be here. I can't blame you. But the
sooner you drink up, the sooner that IV comes out of your
arm."

Dr. Snyder and Peggy McPherson came in at the same time,
laughing and talking like old friends. *They* didn't care. *They*
weren't the guinea pig! Then the nurse was wheeling the pole
with the plastic tube and bottle alongside her bed. She began pre-
paring Lily's arm, still chattering about the bowl games, not
watching what she was doing. Lily tensed. Her throat stuck
when she tried to swallow.

Dr. Snyder was back at the foot of the bed, rubbing her leg this
time but still paying more attention to the nurse than to her.

Coburn worked at the juice cans. "I didn't get any lunch today," she told Lily, "and I'm having an insulin fit." She lined up
the opened cans along the tabletop. "Apple, grape, or orange-
pineapple," she said. "You choose."

Lily clamped her lips together and closed her eyes. It was too
much. She couldn't stand it. She hated them all. They could do
with her body exactly as they pleased, but she wasn't *about* to
participate!

The two doctors left Lily's room shortly after the IV was in
place and dripping.

"There's no sense in my antagonizing her further," Dr. Coburn
told Mrs. McPherson at the nurses' station. "I'll check back
about nine. I'm sure she'll be testing you."

The nurse clicked her ballpoint pen and slipped it into her
pocket. "Any special instructions? I've seen every trick in the
book, but these starvers still manage to surprise me."

"Avoid a power struggle, that's all. It might be a good idea just to keep that bathroom door locked for now. Then she'll have to use the bedpan when she starts urinating again."

"Oh, one more thing..." Dr. Coburn turned back.

"Would you order identical trays for us for lunch tomorrow?" Have Lily choose, if she will. If not, keep the meal skimpy and light. I'll be here a little after twelve."

"Sure thing."

"Thanks." Dr. Coburn waved as she walked down the hall.

Eighteen

Daniel left his car and ran across the hospital parking lot, hurrying to make the last half of the evening visiting hour. He wondered if Lily's mom and dad would still be there. He'd feel uneasy talking to Lily with them in the room.

Inside, following the big arrows to the information desk, he walked lightly, suddenly aware of his noisy boots. He hoped the book he bought for Lily would make up for his not coming sooner. She had been in the hospital for two whole days before he knew about it, and then he got the news secondhand from Erica.

"Mrs. Jamison says Lily has been hospitalized with a blood problem. Heard anything about it?" she'd asked him on the phone.

Daniel hadn't.

"I don't know one thing about Lily's blood problem," Daniel's mother said when he asked her. "And I don't intend to pry. Karen will tell me when she's good and ready."

His folks were so afraid of "prying." My God, he thought, can't you ever risk being misinterpreted? They vehemently denied the stay-in-your-place mentality that was Grandma Perry's standard for happy blacks, but once—just once—he'd like to see his folks rock the boat until someone got wet. He itched to do it himself from time to time.

Daniel approached the circular information desk. His eyes unconsciously singled out the black volunteer from several others working there. Suddenly he grinned: Daniel, the great boat-rocker, rocks again! Who was he to talk?

"May I help you?" she asked.

"Um...yes. Can you tell me which room Lily Jamison's in?"

The girl smiled mechanically as she flipped a set of locator cards. "Oh, I'm sorry. She isn't allowed visitors yet."

"No visitors?" Daniel felt his expression slip.

"None."

"Is she that sick? Or do I have to be her family or something?"

"That I don't know. You could try again in a few days."

"Well..." Daniel looked around, uncertain. Then he held up the paper bag containing the book of Emily Dickinson's poems. "Could you give her this?"

"Certainly. Is your name on it somewhere?"

"No, wait, I'd better write a note...."

He pulled a pen out of his pocket and walked away to one of the lounge chairs, thinking how critical she must be if she couldn't have visitors. Did she have leukemia? He'd thought of that when he first got home. What could he say if she had leukemia? He couldn't *do* anything. What in the world could he say in a note?

"Gal pal," he wrote after giving it some thought, "I still have the poem you wrote for me when I won the track scholarship. I like it better than any of these. Please get well. Yours, Daniel."

Nineteen

Dr. Coburn stopped to talk with Peggy McPherson on the way to Lily's room. It was day four of hospitalization and Lily was still playing a game of wits with everyone.

"I took away her book of poems yesterday...she had it hidden under the bedclothes," McPherson said at the nurses' station. "She had one helluva fit. Made a doughball out of her sandwich and pudding. You should have seen her tray when she got through with it."

Dr. Coburn shook her head.

"Then she called me to clean her up. She insisted on having me do it. All very politely, of course, didn't raise her voice or anything. There's a lot of rage in there, Doctor."

Jessica Coburn patted McPherson's arm. "You're pure patience. What would my skinny girls do without you?"

"Actually," Coburn leaned against the counter, "you needn't be too rigid with Lily. Use your own judgment. Reading a book isn't going to use up that many calories, and once you've made her your enemy..."

"I admit that crossed my mind."

"I'm going to take her onto the sun porch in a wheelchair today. Try another approach," Dr. Coburn said.

"Good luck!"

"Send our trays up when they come, would you, please?"

Lily didn't speak when Dr. Coburn pushed the wheelchair into her room a few minutes later. She just lay there, staring at the ceiling. She clutched the patchwork pillow tight against her chest.

"Let's go somewhere," Dr. Coburn said seductively, patting the back of the wheelchair.

Lily turned to look at her, scowling as much as she dared. "You mean you're going to let me out of this bed?"

"Of course. We agreed, remember? You've gained three pounds."

"And I hate it!"

"Come on, let's celebrate. Need some help getting up?"

Dr. Coburn helped her out of bed and to the bathroom, then into her robe and slippers. Lily tried not to lean on Coburn, but once she had to. "This is so dumb," she muttered. "Do we have to drag this dumb IV with us?"

"That's your dumb lifeline," Coburn said, lifting the tube over and around Lily's head. "Besides, it's the fashion around here. Everybody has one."

In the glassed-in sun-room, where the hospital atmosphere was softened by hanging ferns and bright wicker lounges, Dr. Coburn rolled Lily into position at an empty table so that her back was in the sunlight.

"Does the view suit you?"

Lily turned to look out the window, remembering that the hospital towers overlooked the north end of the university campus. From this top-floor vantage point she could see the roofs of fraternity row, the President's Circle, a snowy stretch of campus that looked like the golf course. Daniel was down there somewhere, sitting in class. . . .

"This is okay," Lily said, trying to keep any hint of enthusiasm out of her voice. *If she knows I like it here, I'll never get to come again.*

Dr. Coburn sat down across from Lily, looking relaxed and easy in the sunlight. She sort of stretched out and closed her eyes. Lily thought she might be fancying a nap for herself.

So today we sit nodding in the sunlight, two old ladies in the nursing home. Zzzzzzz!

Lily looked around at the other patients. Two men were playing checkers, some teenagers in wheelchairs had a backgammon set. The rest were readers and dozers, and there was one snorer who looked as if she might fall out of her chair.

Why isn't Coburn talking? Is she mad at me?

Lily squirmed in the wheelchair, which was anything but comfortable. *Maybe I'll just sit here and die of boredom. That's what they all want. Seventeen-year-old girl gains three pounds and dies of boredom.* Finally, the silence grew nasty. Coburn had no right to ignore her.

"Hey, are you awake?" Lily asked.

"Hmm?" Coburn stirred.

"Did Peggy tell you what I did yesterday?"

Coburn opened her eyes. "What'd you do?"

"They brought me butterscotch pudding when I ordered lime Jell-O. I gooped it all up."

"That made you mad, huh?"

"They can't get anything straight around here!"

"Is that what *really* made you mad yesterday, Lily?"

"No."

"They confiscated your book, didn't they?"

Lily didn't answer. She turned and stared purposefully out the window.

"We all get too zealous sometimes, trying to do the right thing. I think if you feel like reading, you might as well. If you don't turn the pages too vigorously...burn up too many calories..."

Lily pressed her lips together, trying not to smile.

"We ought to make some more plans," Dr. Coburn said. "By Sunday, if you can give up on the 'malts' and be eating regular meals, you might want to invite a friend in to have lunch or dinner with you."

"I'd have to stay in bed, and what fun would that be for anybody?"

"No, wait a minute now. Privileges come with pounds. We talked about all that, remember? You can go down and meet someone in the cafeteria, put the tab on your hospital bill if you like."

"Dr. Coburn, I don't want to gain back all that weight."

"And we don't want you to. We're asking for one pound at a time, just to get you out of danger. A goal of ninety pounds would be acceptable for now. You and I could be out running around the hospital for our noon-hour therapy instead of sitting here dozing. That would be a lot more fun."

Lily smiled then, in spite of herself. What she wouldn't give to be out running again!

"We can set it up any way that sounds comfortable," Coburn went on. "Two more pounds, call a friend. Ten more, we do laps together outside. If your weight's up again tomorrow, you can walk around an hour or two on the floor."

"This is crazy," Lily grumbled. "Privileges for pounds. What if you change your mind...or forget?"

"We'll draw up a contract, make it legal and binding." Dr. Coburn flashed her Girl Scout oath just as their trays arrived.

"It's about time," Coburn said, sounding surly all of a sudden. She studied the tray McPherson handed her. "Oh, no, look here! Strawberry ice cream and I can't stand it."

Lily was confused. "That's what I ordered," she said, half apologizing. "Don't you like strawberry?"

"It gives me hives." Dr. Coburn thrust the plastic container at

McPherson. "Send it down to the kitchen and get me some vanilla."

"Certainly, Dr. Coburn." Peggy McPherson lowered her eyes and hurried away.

"The sandwich looks good, though, " Coburn said as she spread her napkin and took the lid off her coffee. "I'm glad you ordered pita bread. What's in it?"

"Sprouts and chicken," Lily answered, half scared that her psychotherapist wouldn't like that either.

Coburn took a big bite of her sandwich. "Mmm, good. I was starving."

Lily nibbled at the pickle on her plate.

"If you don't like what they bring, make them take it back," Coburn said between bites. "It's your lunch, after all, and you're paying for it."

"I didn't know you could do that."

"Oh, sure. One of my girls made a point of exchanging one or two items a day. She knew a lot about nutrition and just insisted on getting a well-balanced meal."

Lily sipped at her milk, then picked up her pocket bread and looked it over.

"If you can't finish your sandwich, I will," Coburn said as Lily hesitated. "I get so busy I don't eat, and then I get weak and headachy. By two o'clock I'm shaking and mad at everybody."

"I guess you didn't get breakfast today," Lily mumbled.

"Are you going to eat your orange sections?" Coburn asked a minute later.

Lily shrugged. "I sort of like them."

Dr. Coburn ate her own dish of mandarin oranges halfway through her sandwich, then kept her eye on Lily's fruit, finally asking if Lily wanted to share some of hers. "I have a passion for those," she apologized. "You can have my black olive and celery, if you like. Want to trade?"

Lily gave away five orange sections, keeping four for herself.

"Eating gets to be such a formal activity in some families," Coburn said. "Meals ought to be warm, happy, sharing times in my opinion."

They talked about school then, and how soon Lily could start doing assignments again. Coburn wanted to know if Lily had a friend who'd bring her work to the hospital when the time came.

Lily told her about Eda Mae Rolphe and her amazing faculties of retention. Eda Mae was in four of her classes, including English and Latin. Before she knew it, Lily had eaten all her sandwich. She speared a pickled beet with her fork, hiding the second one behind her lettuce leaf so Coburn wouldn't get to it before she did.

"Here's your ice cream," McPherson announced. Obviously, she liked being Coburn's lackey. "Anything else?"

Lily held up her own ice cream. "I'd really rather have chocolate than this. Could you get me a chocolate?"

"You bet."

Lily smiled and covered her mouth with her napkin. She and Coburn looked at one another conspiratorially.

"See?" Coburn whispered as the nurse turned her back. "All you have to do is assert yourself."

Twenty

Lily had a hard time forcing down food when Dr. Coburn wasn't there, but she desperately wanted off the IV. Her left arm was swollen, alternately painful and numb, and dragging "Frieda" around was a monstrous chore. Now that she was up each day, Frieda the IV Pole went with her to the bathroom, down the hall to the library, to the vending machine, everywhere. They were like twins. "Identical twins," the fat night nurse joked, laughing herself silly over it. Lily hated her. Caroline Pritchart was her name, and she was sadistic.

Every night when she came on duty, Pritchart did a number on Lily's room to see if she was hiding her food instead of eating it.

"Why would I hide food in the hem of the drapes?" Lily asked.

"It's been done!" Pritchart said, pinching the corners of each panel. Then she'd poke her fingers into the pot of chrysanthemums, shake out Lily's slippers, run her hand inside the pillowcase, and frisk out the bedclothes.

You're giving me ideas, Lily thought the first time it happened. After that, she looked forward to the ritual inspection. It was her evening entertainment. She wondered if she should store some green beans somewhere to keep the game going, but Pritchart never lost heart.

The last joyful service from ol' Caroline before she went off duty was the weighing-in. For some reason, it had to be done at 6:00 A.M., like weighing patients any later would jeopardize their health.

"Time to void!" Pritchart would yell up and down the hall. At six in the morning Lily couldn't even *find* the bathroom, but Pritchart was always there to assist. Then off they went, Frieda tagging along, to be weighed on the free-arm balance scale "accurate to the nearest tenth of a kilogram."

It was obvious to Lily that Pritchart had more regard for the scales than for her patients. She handled the weights with such love and tenderness, Lily felt an awful urge each time to give Pritchart's Pet a swift kick in the accuracy. She never did, of course, being barefooted.

In spite of the miseries of hospital life, Lily had started to feel better. She was trying to cooperate, trying to finish part of each meal, though the guilt after eating even a small bowl of cereal was enormous.

Even so, eating in the hospital was easier than eating at home. So long as she showed a gain each day, nobody hassled her. No one cared how she ate the food or how long it took. No one sat there watching her chew, making sure she swallowed. Somehow the pressure was off.

The meals were brought in and removed without comment, though she once caught McPherson writing down everything she'd left on her dinner tray that day.

"We have to keep track," was all McPherson would say.

They measured her urine, too. Lily knew that was why she had to use the "witch's hat" whenever she went to the john. But the measuring and keeping track didn't bother Lily. The daily weight gain did. And *that* Pritchart tried her damnedest to conceal.

Since she wasn't allowed to exercise, Lily found comfort in doing "mental gymnastics," as she thought of them privately. After each meal she'd lie down on her bed and go through the old, familiar routines—vaulting, working out on the uneven bar, the balance beam. The fantasy took on new embellishments as she went along. Soon there were crowds to watch her perform, judges to admire her. They'd describe her with such phrases as "sparkling performance" and "amazing consistency." At the end, she'd dazzle everyone with an intricate floor exercise that left her face glistening and her heart pounding. Often, she noticed, her heart really *would* be pounding. Lily was convinced that rigorous daydreaming would burn up some of the extra calories she was getting.

Finally, come Saturday, the IV was removed and all Lily could think about was running again. Her body ached for exercise. She even tried jogging in place in the bathroom, but McPherson caught her at it and made her quit.

"I'm rotting from the inside out!" she had moaned, following her nurse down the hall. "I'm starting to decay. I *am*! I need to *move*!"

"Doctor's orders," McPherson said for the hundredth time She had no sympathy!

The bad news came on Sunday morning at the weighing-in, when Pritchart told Lily, in a burst of generosity, that she'd gained over six pounds in eight days of hospitalization.

"My gosh," Lily gasped. "Eighty-four pounds! I'm obese!"

Then she remembered. Coburn had promised she could stop at ninety pounds. She had that in writing!

Lily also remembered that she had a reward coming. The big payoff for a five-pound gain, Coburn and she had agreed, was for Lily to invite a friend to have a meal with her in the cafeteria. Downstairs. In the "real world."

Still grumbling to Pritchart about the grossness of her body, Lily nonetheless found herself brightening at the prospect of an hour of freedom away from the fifth floor. She'd earned the privilege. Why shouldn't she take it? Besides, she was sick of sucking on straws. All of a sudden it was a big deal, eating in the cafeteria, choosing her meal from behind a glass case.

After breakfast Lily showered and washed her hair. She used her curling iron for the first time in a week. All the while she was wondering whom she should call. Or more accurately—who would *come*. Daniel was her first choice, of course, but she couldn't ask him. He'd probably be spending the day with Kimberly Reems.

Lily dug for a pair of knee socks in the bag lying open on her bed. She tried picturing them together, Daniel and the gorgeous tall girl with the teeth. Kimberly was much too sophisticated-looking for Daniel. She was probably older, too. Why didn't she pick on someone her own age? Lily sat down on the edge of her bed, smoothing her socks across her lap, staring at nothing. She wondered if he'd kissed her yet. And how he'd kissed her... and held her... and what they talked about when they were alone.

Lily pulled on her sock with a yank. If she couldn't ask Daniel to come to eat with her, she could at least talk with him on the phone, couldn't she? She had to thank him for the poetry book. He had tried to see her that once. So far as she knew, he was the only one....

Lily was strangely relieved, a little later, when Mrs. Perry told her on the phone that Daniel had taken his grandmother to church. That meant he wasn't with *her*. Not right now, anyway.

"Thanks, Mrs. Perry," she had said. "Tell him I love the Emily Dickinson."

Lily leaned against the partitioning of the phone booth, feeling her anticipation slip away. She didn't really want to see anyone else. Erica *might* come. She knew Franklin Rogers would, but he was so embarrassingly fat. Feeling defeated, Lily walked slowly back to her room. She'd have dinner in the cafeteria by herself.

Daniel stood in the doorway of Lily's room for a full twenty seconds before she looked up from her magazine and saw him. She was sitting cross-legged on her bed, wearing gray slacks and a pink sweater. Her hair had fallen over half her face, which was in profile to him, so at first he wasn't sure if the girl on the bed was Lily. Then she looked up.

"Daniel!" She dropped the *Runner's World,* swung her legs over the side of the bed. "Did I *wish* you here?"

He laughed and walked in. "You must have. I've been shaking with Lily-vibes all day." He stuck out two unsteady hands.

"Oh, you!" she said, grabbing and wrenching his fingers back. He managed a pained expression as they scuffled and laughed. Daniel was relieved to have such a terrific welcome, though he could hardly believe this skeleton with the cold hands was Lily Jamison.

She started talking at once. "I can't tell you how glad I am to see you. Daniel, this place is so borrrrring! Honest, I was about to do myself in, fall on a fork or something."

Daniel hooted.

"So what's the scoop? When do you get out of here?" he asked as she hung his parka in a closet.

"Who knows? You could say I'm merely living from pound to pound. When I get in the nineties, maybe I can go home. Truth is, I gave up all my rights when I checked in here."

She looked bonier than ever to Daniel—her cheeks hollow, her eyes overlarge for her face. Of course, he hadn't seen her for a while. Not since the Jamisons' open house, really.

[145]

"You're looking better already," he lied, "so you must be getting better. Gosh, it won't be long until you're back in the circle, making my life miserable again."

Lily grinned. "Yeah, I suppose." She sent an uneasy glance around the room. "Well...there's nothing to do here, that's the whole trouble. You want a can of pop?"

"No, I just ate dinner."

"Me, too. I got to eat with the 'normals' tonight."

"Oh, yeah?"

"In the cafeteria. It was my first 'outing.' Some big deal, huh?" Suddenly her face brightened. "Say, you want to see something neat?"

Lily walked to the door, looked in both directions, then motioned him to follow her.

"I'm not supposed to leave the fifth floor by myself," she whispered, "so I won't. I'll leave it with you."

"Where we going?" he whispered back.

"Upstairs to the sun-room. They have a game cupboard and stuff. It's much nicer than my cell."

They had to wait at the elevator, where Lily made sure Daniel stood between her and the central desk. She needn't have worried. The only nurse on duty was so busy with her computer she didn't look up.

Slick as a greased doorknob, they slipped into the elevator and headed for the eighth floor.

Daniel aimed a gun at his head: "If I get you in trouble..."

"No chance. Everything's lax during visiting hours."

Upstairs in the lounge, Lily led Daniel to the wall of windows which overlooked the lighted university grounds.

"I wanted to show you the view," she said, sounding almost shy.

"Very nice." Daniel nodded and took it all in.

They stood there a while, looking down at the scattering of lights marking the buildings and walkways and drives of the campus. A bus entered the President's Circle and stopped. Two miniature people got out.

"I've eaten lunch up here before," Lily said. "I tried to imagine where you were that day, which building you'd be in."

He pulled her over next to him. "See the administration building there at the top of the circle?" She nodded. "Go left, there's a brick building, then there's a long, flat, barrackslike affair. That's where I *live*. I'll wave at you tomorrow."

Lily giggled. "I wish I could trade places with you."

"No, you don't. I'm on very shaky ground. I'm going to fail my physics lab sure as shit if I don't start catching on."

"You? You've never failed anything in your life!"

They drifted toward a chartreuse wicker sofa and sat down facing each other. Daniel's glance took in the chess players and a man reading in a wheelchair beyond them. He wondered if visitors were even allowed in this lounge. Returning to Lily, he found her eyes full of questions.

"Is physics that tough?" she asked in a quiet voice.

"It's not just physics...I'm not doing very well in school. I wasn't any star at Stanford, either."

"I can't believe that."

"Neither can my folks, but they're trying not to let on." He chuckled, pulled his upper lip tight across his teeth. "They go around like this"—he pointed to himself—"stiff upper lip."

Lily laughed.

"Of course, Grandma has a little trouble stiffening hers."

They both cracked up over that.

"Okay, Daniel Perry, you're just pulling my leg."

"No, I'm not. Honest, I'm thinking about dropping out. I was going to wait until spring quarter, but—"

[147]

"*Daniel*!"

"I just can't cut it."

"But you *can*! You're so smart! What happened?"

They leaned close now, faces earnest in the dim light of a floor lamp, as Daniel tried to explain how miserable he'd been studying physics and advanced math and all the related prerequisites for computer science.

"It's not my thing, but I listened to my dad, you know? My folks have really scratched, both of them, to get where they are. They want an easier life for us kids. 'Computer science,' my dad's been saying like a broken record. Well, it's just not my bag."

"And you're the one who has to decide...something I've been learning the hard way," Lily added under her breath.

Daniel sighed. "It's not the end of the world. I can't blame them because I took a wrong turn."

Lily shook her head sympathetically, her face reflecting his anxiety. *She's still an intense listener,* Daniel thought, *but why am I spilling my guts to her? She's the one who needs cheering. What's the matter with me?* He turned away, exhaled noisily.

"Hey, look, Lily, I'm sorry. Forget I said anything."

"Why should I do that?"

"Because I don't want you to worry about me. Besides," he forced a cheerful tone, "if I do drop out, I'll be jumping back in again in the fall, trying something else."

"Daniel, I feel terrible! I didn't have any idea."

"No, hey, please, it's not going to get me down. I maybe wasted some time, that's all, but then...you know, so have you." He saw her react. "You know what I'm saying—maybe we needed some time out, you and me. We steam-rollered through high school, knocking 'em dead, both of us. Now maybe it's our turn for a little 'reality therapy.' So we hit a snag, so what? I'm going to be okay, aren't you?" Her forehead gathered into a knot.

"Oh, Daniel, I wish I were as sure as you. I'm so scared of going back home, living in that house with them. I can eat better here, but something terrible happens to me even thinking how it was before."

Daniel made a hopeless gesture. "Anorexia...man, it's so weird! I sure don't understand it."

"Do you think *I* do?"

"Is your shrink any good?" Daniel asked abruptly.

"I like her all right. You know, she's okay, but I don't know if she can change the way I am. Maybe nobody can. Maybe I don't want them to." She stared at the thin-skinned hands in her lap. "I'm scared, Daniel."

"Now, listen—" He leaned close, making her look at him. "You're going to get well. You're going to be your ornery old self again. You'll be eating right and gaining weight and you'll be healthy, just like in the 'olden days.'" He had taken her icy hands and held them tight between his own. "You hear these direct orders I'm giving you?"

Lily nodded.

"Okay?"

She gave him a very small, very tentative smile.

"Hey, look what I brought with me." He gave her hands a squeeze as he set them back in her lap, then dug into his rear pocket for a deck of cards. "How about a little poker? Twenty-one, five-card stud? You feel up to a game?" He shuffled the cards into his left hand. "Figured I might just beat the socks off you tonight, like I used to."

That struck sparks in her eyes.

"You, sir, have a slightly *im*perfect memory."

Daniel snorted.

Once seated at a nearby table, the battle was on: a few flashy shuffles, Lily cutting the deck, Daniel dealing, Lily asking, "Can

[149]

you loan me some money?" Daniel answering, "Don't I always?" More laughing and bantering as they sorted their hands.

By the time visiting hours were over, Lily was richer by forty-five cents, a ballpoint pen, and the deck of cards itself. She'd not only stripped Daniel of all his nickels and dimes, she'd also called him a sore loser and a cheat and several other impolite names. He didn't care. He left the hospital whistling, his step lighter than it had been in days.

Twenty-one

The last thing Lily expected Monday morning when she returned from the hospital library was to find company waiting for her. Well, Coburn wasn't exactly *company*. Wearing a red car coat the color of her cheeks, she sat perched on the edge of Lily's bed, flipping through a new *Seventeen* she'd apparently brought with her. Lily smiled, knowing now what it was she liked most about her psychiatrist: She never, ever followed a script.

"Put on your coat," Coburn said after Lily spoke.

"How come?"

"It's forty-six degrees out there and the sun's shining. We're taking a turn around the building."

"No lie?" Lily grinned. "Running?"

"Walking."

Outside, Coburn linked arms with Lily and they started out in step. "It's a half mile around," she said. "Can you make it?"

"I'd go six times if you'd let me!" Lily filled her lungs with fresh air. The outdoors smelled so good.

"Say, I understand you've gained a little weight. I'm really very pleased."

Lily made a face.

"Did you ask a friend up to visit yesterday?"

"I went down to the cafeteria and ate by myself."

"You did?"

"I couldn't decide who to call. But guess what? Daniel came to see me without having to be invited. Daniel Perry, remember?"

"Your neighbor, right?"

"...and my best friend. But I wasn't going to call and ask him."

"Didn't you think he'd want to see you?"

"I don't know, he has a girlfriend...you know what I mean ...he's busy, and he's a *college man,* as my mother likes to point out."

They turned the northwestern corner of the building and faced into the wind. Lily put up her hood.

'Well, it's good to have someone to share your miseries with. Is Daniel that kind of friend?"

"Yes, when I give him a chance." Lily frowned, feeling a jab of guilt for the way she'd been treating him. "But he's a very strong person. He doesn't let things get to him the way I do."

"I guess you feel weak compared to someone like Daniel."

"Compared to Daniel, I'm a blade of grass."

Coburn made a megaphone with her hand. "Step right up, folks. Walk on me!"

"Really," Lily said laughing, her breath making frosty puffs in the air.

"Where does Daniel come up with all that self-esteem?"

"Is that what it is?"

Coburn released Lily's arm and they both searched for their pockets. "I forgot to mention the windchill factor, didn't I?"

They walked a while without talking, heads down. Finally, Lily looked sideways at Jessica Coburn. "Daniel's black, did you know that?"

"No, you never mentioned it."

"You know what else? His whole family has self-esteem." Lily walked slowly, absorbed in what she was saying.

"Lily, you really admire Daniel and his family. Is there a big difference between their life-style and yours — as families go, that is?"

"Gosh, yes, we're totally different."

"How? Describe Daniel's family for me. What are the Perrys like?"

"Well, to begin with, there are three kids in the family, and Grandma Perry, who lives with them. The father teaches at the university. And Florence Perry is a social worker at Family Services. Oh, yes, and Trinh's adopted. She's part Vietnamese. Now ...what else can I say?"

Coburn waited.

"Sometimes they're too noisy for me, I guess. Our family's quiet, mostly."

"You mean noisy with yelling and screaming?"

"No...you know...they tease a lot, clown around...something's always going on over there."

"Busy noise."

"Yeah. Maybe the biggest thing is that they're very affectionate. That's what you'd notice first. Skipper's five and he's always hanging onto Daniel, tore his back jeans pocket off once from hanging on so much. That was the summer before Daniel left for Stanford." Lily remembered Daniel's astonishment when it happened and how they'd laughed.

"Skipper is Juju's age, then—"

"And they're thick as thieves, those two. Juju *lives* over there."

"So when Daniel left for college, you were sort of out in the cold."

"Yeah, I guess you could say that. I was pretty depressed."

"But you didn't complain about it?"

"Oh, you know," Lily scrunched up her shoulders. "I'd been elected cheerleader and I was on the gymnastics team. I was popular and successful, supposedly. Besides my parents are always upset if they think I'm upset. Vicious cycle."

"Let's rest a minute," Coburn said as they reached the south face of the hospital. "This wing houses the medical library. Did you know that? I used to study outside here on nice days." She led Lily to a low retaining wall that caught the morning sunlight. "We're in no hurry, are we?"

Lily was cold, but she *never* wanted to go in.

"So Daniel's family is noisy and affectionate and yours is quiet and affectionate."

"Ha!" Lily said. "Our family is not affectionate. Not anymore."

They dangled their legs, heels banging against the cement wall. Lily began to feel that Coburn was her own age, that she was her friend, not her psychiatrist, and that they were having a serious talk, the way friends do.

"When did everything change for the Jamisons?" Coburn asked.

"I don't know, but it did."

"I like the way you describe Daniel's family. You have a nice sensitivity, you pick up on things. Thinking along those same lines, can you tell me more specifically how your family operates?"

Lily could feel a smirk developing. Did Coburn want the truth? *We lie a lot and sneak around and hurt one another's feelings...but we pretend that everything's okay...we're very good at that....*

"Lily," Coburn went on when she didn't answer, "we've talked mostly about you personally in our sessions. You know, your feelings, your nutritional needs, and so on. We're going to shift the focus in your therapy now. I need to see Lily Jamison in a family context. Do you know what I mean?"

Lily wasn't sure.

"Go back to what you said about showing affection. Let's explore that a minute. I'm wondering if your parents are still affectionate with Juju—at her age."

"Sometimes my dad is, but not like he was with me. We were really very tight when I was little. He doesn't pay that much attention to Juju. She's kind of spoiled."

"I love the pictures she sent you," Coburn said, stiffening her arms and fingers into a stick figure. Lily had taped Juju's drawings around the room—the fats and the skinnies—plus one purple fingerpainting on which Lily had written, "Move over, Picasso." The nurses were all bidding on that one, all except Pritchart, who said it looked like an eggplant casserole.

"I miss Juju more than I thought I would," Lily admitted. "At home we don't get along very well."

"From what you've told me, I gather that your mother has a harder time expressing affection than your father."

"Understatement," Lily muttered.

Suddenly the cement grew hard. Lily could feel the cold coming right through her jeans. She slipped off the retaining wall and leaned against it instead.

Coburn went on talking. "I've heard you say your mother's the boss at your house. Does that mean she makes decisions for your father, too?"

"She makes all the decisions."

The way an optical illusion pops in front of the eyes, Coburn-the-Friend became Coburn-the-Psychiatrist again, and Lily felt cheated. "I don't want to talk about her. We always end up talking about my mother. Maybe I should go home and she should come up here. You'd probably like her a lot." Lily looked back at the sidewalk.

Dr. Coburn stood and they started walking again. She took hold of Lily's arm, but Lily wished she hadn't.

"Wednesday you and I will be eating lunch here with your family," she said, calm as anything.

The news detonated inside Lily. She pulled away sharply.

"How come? Why are we doing that? My dad won't take off work, he never does."

"He said he'd be here."

"Why are they coming up here?"

"We'll be eating a cafeteria lunch in my conference room on the ground floor, so don't order a tray that day. Okay?"

Lily felt a tightening in her stomach. She wasn't ready to see them yet. She didn't want them here. It would ruin everything!

"Juju...Is she coming, too?"

"I hope so."

"I won't be able to eat. Don't expect me to eat anything!"

"Lily," Coburn said, "I must see you with your family. You may be the identified patient, but they need help as much as you do. You have the symptoms, but the illness belongs to the whole family."

Lily stared at Dr. Coburn.

"Yours is what we call a psychosomatic family. You've told me that yourself a number of times."

"I have?"

Coburn smiled. She gave Lily a squeeze. "Come on now, don't look so somber. I'll be right there with you."

Lily wasn't so sure about anything now. She felt diluted. She never dreamed she'd have to share Coburn with *them*.

She shivered, ducking her head against the wind, which suddenly zeroed right into her bones.

Twenty-two

Lily ate nothing Monday after Dr. Coburn left and very little on Tuesday. When Pritchart weighed her early Wednesday morning, they discovered she'd actually lost a pound.

"I'm not trying to lose," Lily protested when the nurse clucked her tongue. "I just can't swallow, that's all. I told McPherson, and I told you last night. I can't make the food go down anymore."

"You were doing so well," Pritchart said.

Didn't they believe her when she said she couldn't eat? Why didn't they listen to her? She'd tell Dr. Coburn when she saw her at lunchtime. She'd pay attention.

It was nearing eleven when Lily and her psychiatrist stepped out of the elevator on Level One. Lily could see her family waiting with Dr. Snyder at the end of the hall near the cafeteria. As soon as Juju saw Lily, she broke away from her mother and came pounding down the hospital corridor to grab her sister's hand.

"I get to eat with you," she squealed, swinging Lily's arm in the air.

"Says who, little monkey?"

"Says me!"

Lily's hand tightened on her sister's as they walked along.

Holding on for dear life was what she was doing. The idea of Coburn meeting with her whole family was terrifying. Now she had to worry about *them* as well as about herself.

"Good morning," the doctors said as they met, including everyone with their congenial smiles and nods.

Suddenly, surprising her as much as it did him, Lily threw her arms around her father's neck and started to cry.

"It's okay, honey...." He held her close, patting her head. Finally, laughing, he pried her loose and held her at arm's length. "You've got some strength back, I can tell that."

"We've missed you so much," her mother said, tears shining in her eyes, "but you're looking much better, darling."

"I got to sleep in your bed once," Juju piped up.

Lily wiped her cheeks, throwing her sister a sideways look at the same time. Her father handed her his handkerchief.

Then Dr. Coburn was ushering them inside her large conference room, explaining that Dr. Snyder had to get back to his office and could stay only a few minutes. "Find places to sit, everyone."

They all seated themselves at the round table, Howard Jamison holding a chair out for Lily between him and his wife. Juju climbed onto the one next to her father. The doctors sat side by side in the two remaining chairs.

Lily caught herself twisting her fingers, but stopped at once. She took a deep breath. She wondered if she looked as stiff as her mother, who was busy arranging her skirt and her legs just so. Lily noticed she'd had her hair tipped in the past week. She looked stunning: "tastefully understated," like the clothes she illustrated. Lily's eyes slid over her own rust-colored sweater and jeans, the same outfit she'd worn to the hospital days ago.

Dr. Snyder was talking to her parents about her improvement, the change in her vital signs, the weight she'd gained. She forced herself to pay attention.

"But"—he paused and smiled directly at her—"we're not out of the woods yet."

Lily returned to studying the seam line on her jeans. *That's where I'd like to be right now, in the woods behind our house. With Daniel. Finding squirrel tracks in the snow. Daniel has such a good eye for little creatures. He always spots them before I do.*

Then Dr. Snyder was excusing himself, after which Jessica Coburn pulled her chair nearer the table. Juju started fidgeting, causing Karen to shake her head and frown. Lily's throat went dry. They all sat there, trying not to look at one another.

"You know what?" Coburn leaned across the table toward Juju. "If I lit a match right now, the tension in this room would blow us sky high." Juju quit fidgeting immediately, hoping for an explosion, no doubt.

"Let's loosen up a little," Coburn said, her hands flying around. "This is not the Last Supper, it's the first lunch."

She patted Juju's cheek. "Shall we play a game? I know Juju likes games." She walked across the room, rummaged around in a desk drawer, returned to the conference table.

"First of all, join hands." She reached out toward Karen. "Sort of lean in on the table, everyone. Juju, you'll have to get up on your knees, I'll bet. There! The idea is to keep this golf ball rolling without having to break contact. Whoever lets it drop through to the floor has to go pick up the menus. Any questions? . . . Ready?"

Juju whooped as the ball came toward her first, but she stopped it under her chest.

"Good girl!" Coburn said and laughed.

Lily blocked it next, snapping it across to Coburn with the inside of her elbow. It rolled back toward Karen.

"Oh, no!" Karen said with a little shriek. She broke hands with Lily to catch it.

"Foul!"

"Oh, dear, what do I do now?"

"Start it out again," Coburn said. "We'll let that one go."

Howard blocked it twice in a row, then sent it off with such force it slipped through between Juju and Dr. Coburn and hit the floor with a thud. Juju groaned. Everyone else laughed.

"That's what we get for playing with a pro!" Coburn said. "Well done there, Howard. You must have played elbow tennis before."

He grinned. "Not exactly."

Coburn stood and took Juju's hand. "Come on, we lost. It's up to us."

As soon as they were gone, Lily's father reached down and picked up the ball. "Elbow tennis... Is this what I'm giving up half a day's work for?"

"I'm sure there's some point to it," Karen said, sounding impatient in spite of her words.

"When can I come home?" Lily whispered. "Did she say when I'm getting out?"

Her father didn't answer. He spoke to her mother instead. "She didn't need hospitalization in the first place, if you ask me."

"She's gained five pounds. That's something."

"Mother!"

"I'm sorry, but I've been hearing this every day since you left. Don't you believe Dr. Snyder, Howard? Even her color's better."

"She could have gained five pounds at home if she'd set her mind to do it."

"But she wouldn't," her mother said crossly.

Lily was invisible. Their words were flying right past her nose as if she wasn't there.

Then Coburn was back, handing out menus and little order blanks, telling Juju she could return them when they were filled out. Lily felt better with Coburn in the room.

"Oh, look," Karen said brightly, "they have a seafood salad. Doesn't that sound good, Lily?"

"There's a lot more than seafood to choose from," Howard said.

Lily looked from one to the other.

"I think we should change our seating here," Dr. Coburn suggested, "so you two can talk without Lily in the middle. Parents have things they need to discuss..."

Lily stood and traded places with her mother, who seemed ready to protest but didn't.

"Why don't you have the roast beef sandwich, Lily?" her father said. "That's what I'm ordering."

"Lily," Dr. Coburn interrupted, "how old are you?"

She looked at her doctor quizzically. "I'm seventeen."

"And you, Juju, how old are you?"

Juju sat up straight. "Five. And almost six."

"Hmm." Coburn looked at Juju. "No one's telling you what to order, but both parents are trying to order for their seventeen-year-old. I'm confused here."

"Well," Karen said, smiling, "under the circumstances—"

"—we worry about Lily, not Juju," Howard finished her sentence. "Juju eats everything."

"I think a seventeen-year-old girl can select her own lunch. Unless you'd rather play 'trade-off,' of course. Some of my families like to do that. If one of you wants to order for Lily, then Lily gets to order for you. Both then agree to eat what the other chooses."

"No!" Lily and her mother said at once.

I'd do it if I dared. Lily could just imagine her mother gagging down an oversized lunch of superfattening foods! Right now her own appetite was zero. Nothing on the menu looked good. In desperation, she checked the boxes for cottage cheese, lime

Jell-O, rolled turkey breast. She hoped the meal didn't automatically include milk.

"No drink, Lily?" Her mother was reading over her shoulder.

"Lily," Coburn stood up this time, "let's move you again. You're still too close to your mother. She won't let you grow up here today."

Karen Jamison looked rebuffed.

"Besides, Juju is the one who needs some help with the menu. Come over here, Lily, where you can give your sister a hand."

Looking pleased, Juju handed her order blank to Lily.

It took a while, plus a few more words from Coburn about "age-appropriate tasks," but lunches were decided on at last, and Juju proudly carried the orders away in a little basket Coburn gave her.

"Howard, let's start with you today," Dr. Coburn said. "Last week when we met together without the kids, we agreed on certain ground rules for these sessions. We also talked a little about the dysfunctioning family. You wanted to know how this family could have produced eating problems such as Lily's. Have you thought any more about that?"

"Well, yes... quite a lot, in fact... but I haven't come up with any answers."

"You're the head of this household, so I'll ask you first to describe how this family functions."

Howard took his time formulating an answer. Finally, he nodded toward his wife. "She runs the show on the domestic side of things. I have to admit, most of the time, things run pretty smoothly around home. I mostly concentrate on the business."

Karen spoke up. "We really don't have any problems, marital or otherwise. We're a very close family. This is the only thing we've come up against that we couldn't handle. It's very unsettling."

Coburn nodded sympathetically. "Well," she spread her hands, "no family lives in perfect harmony. It's normal to fight occasionally. Let's start with that—the way you settle disagreements that do arise. Does one of you usually give in to the other?"

"The only arguments we have are over Lily," her mother said.

Dr. Coburn turned to Lily. "Is that true?"

"The only time they argue out loud is over me," she said softly.

"Would you repeat that?" Coburn said. "I couldn't hear you."

"They fight without words a lot," Lily said louder. "I hate that."

Howard gestured toward his wife. "She's the one who uses the silent treatment. That's not my style."

"I happen to think peace at home is worth the price you pay for it, that's all. I'm not the scrapper Lily's father would like me to be."

Coburn smiled. "We're talking *about* each other here, and that's one of the rules we don't want to break, remember? Tell *him*, Karen. Tell your husband how you feel...go ahead, look at one another...turn your chairs so you can talk. Right! There you go."

Lily's parents laughed nervously as they turned their chairs to face one another.

"Now, Howard, back to you. How would you like your wife to behave when you disagree?"

"I'd like you to get things out in the open, Karen."

She shook her head. "I don't think you really mean that. You never accept criticism in a nice way."

"And you think *you* do?"

Lily helped Juju squeeze back in beside her, secretly pleased to hear her parents go at it in public. She and Juju sat there listening, her sister looking at her from time to time, not sure about what

[163]

was going on. It was like being in a theater, watching two actors in rehearsal, only they were her parents and they were deadly serious.

Finally, when her mother got back to Lily's refusal to eat as the cause of all their tensions, Lily sensed she was going to be involved again, but it didn't happen quite yet.

"Karen," Dr. Coburn observed, "you seem to be a person of many talents. From what I gather, you're a gifted artist, a gourmet cook, a first-class manager. You have all this wonderful ability, and yet I'm getting this message that you feel unappreciated in this family...."

Mrs. Jamison bit her upper lip in a nervous sort of reflex action.

"Do you feel the children appreciate what you do for them?"

"I think Lily resents me."

"Have you asked her why she feels that way? Or *if* she does? Maybe you can ask her...here...today...."

But Karen didn't look at Lily. Her torrent of words was directed at the therapist. "I can't tell you how much she's hurt me, Dr. Coburn. She's uncommunicative, she's sullen...as cold as any human being I've ever known...."

"Better be careful," Howard said under his breath, "You'll be describing yourself."

"I'm describing my older daughter!" Karen said, turning on him. "And Howard's said the same thing!" She sounded near tears.

"So where did Lily learn all this oddball eating?" He moved to face Dr. Coburn. "Lily naturally spends her time with her mother when I'm gone on business. Karen's been dieting all her life, but when Lily...when *she* goes overboard and ends up starving herself...look at them both," he said, pointing. "Karen won't tolerate one extra pound on her frame, and her daughter's growing up to be just like her."

Just then Coburn excused herself and took Juju to a corner

desk, where she proceeded to give her some paper and crayons.

"Would you draw a picture for me? Of your whole family? Can you get four people on one sheet? I'd like a nice picture to take home today." She gave Juju a hug before rejoining them at the table.

"Let's go on," Coburn continued. "Can you see what's happening? Here you are—handsome, intelligent, well-educated adults—and you're still talking *about* one another, not *to* one another. You're not communicating at all. And Lily, who's the subject of this discussion, is given no chance to rebut. We've changed her seat twice, but she's still there, planted solidly between you. She's holding this family together. Her illness is the cement here. And it will be...unless the family structure changes."

Karen sat forward, her long fingers trembling on the arms of the chair. "Would you explain what you mean? Why do we need to accommodate when Lily's the sick one? I just don't understand that."

"All right. Let me try to help you. Families of anorectics are heavily into maintaining the status quo. Issues that threaten change are sidestepped. We see this in your husband's insistence that he has no part in Lily's problem—he's a businessman, who leaves raising the kids up to you, right? So he's free of guilt, okay? The anorectic herself, blocked in every other attempt to reach her parents with her need for independence, uses her illness as a way to communicate. Why should she give that up?" Coburn paused. "You see, the anorectic family entering treatment has some really difficult tasks ahead of it. If Lily is to change, everyone else must change. We know"—and here Coburn punched her forefinger against the table, making her point—"we *know* that when the family organization is changed, the anorectic child improves greatly." She looked at each of them in turn. "It's worth a few fights, some hurt feelings, don't you think?

"All right. That's the longest speech I want to make today.

Therapy takes time, and there's pain involved. Before change comes discovery. That's what we're doing now, trying to discover how you relate to one another within the family unit."

Lily began to understand a little. Families *do* have a structure. Like a cardboard box or something. If one side caves in, the whole thing changes shape. That made sense.

Dr. Coburn leaned back, her expressive hands folded on the table. "Now, Lily...how does this family work as you see it? How do you fit in?"

Lily felt her cheeks grow warm. It was easier being talked about than talking. She didn't know what to say, now that she had the chance.

"What made you starve yourself?" her mother prompted. "Are you trying to tell Daddy and me something, is that it?"

"Lily's supposed to do the talking," her father said.

"She probably can't express what she feels, Howard. I know how that is."

Dr. Coburn shook her head. "Is this what happens to you at home, Lily?"

She nodded.

"Do your parents listen any better to Juju than they do to you?"

"Yes. She screams if no one pays attention."

"Did you ever try screaming?"

Lily smiled at Coburn's ridiculous question. "Of course not."

"Never?"

"I can't remember."

"Lily has always had beautiful manners," her mother said. "We're very proud of the way she conducts herself, aren't we, dear?"

Her father stroked his moustache, nervously, the way he did before a tennis match. "She never gave us a minute's anxiety... until this."

"I think Lily could speak up if she had a little more space."

Dr. Coburn was up and gesturing like a traffic cop once again. "Turn your chairs around, you two. That's right, all the way around."

"With our backs to you?" Howard asked. Lily winced. He sounded amused, and the look he gave Karen said, "Here we go again." *She* trusted Coburn. Why couldn't he?

"Now, Lily, I'm asking your parents not to speak for you, or interpret what you say in any way. Start wherever you like and tell us about Lily Jamison as a member of this family. If they interrupt, you have my permission to scream."

Lily pressed her lips tight to keep from smiling. Then she began.

"Like Daddy says, I guess I take after my mother most." She hesitated, knowing she was bound to hurt one of them. "But sometimes... I'd rather be more like my dad. I knew, all the time I was growing up, that I had to make both of them happy. You see, he expects me to be like him, and she expects me to be like her. I always thought I had to do both. Well, now I'm older, and I don't want to be a carbon copy of anyone. I want to be me, but when I'm *me*, I'm afraid they don't like me very much." Her voice trailed off. "I guess that sounds dumb."

Lily waited, listening to Juju's crayon pressing hard and fast on the paper and wished she were in the corner drawing pictures.

"Go ahead," Coburn said quietly. "What you're saying is not dumb."

"I think"—Lily sighed—"I think I want some of Juju's privileges. I was the one who grew up with all the rules. I had so many 'shalts' and 'shalt not's' I walked around with a guilty conscience all the time. I knew I was never as good or as smart as they thought I was. To make sure *he* liked me, I had to be a child tennis prodigy. For her, I always had to be a perfect little lady. If I didn't bring home A's on every report card, I knew they'd both quit being proud of me."

Coburn reached over and touched Lily. "One thing we try to

improve in therapy is the way we communicate. Seems a little sneaky, when we're all sitting here together, for you and me to be talking about your folks. Tell them how you feel, why don't you?"

"Okay." Lily lifted her chin. "All right, I will. Mom, you want me to be elegant and beautiful and act like an angel all the time. I can't live up to that. Besides, you re not happy, no matter what I do. I'm not happy myself! You never let me choose my clothes or my classes at school. I'm supposed to go to your college and join *your* sorority." Lily's face contorted as anger flooded through her. "Most of all, I wish you'd stop choosing my friends!"

"Lily," Karen said, swinging around, "when did I ever say anything, except with Daniel, who's obviously—"

"Shut up!" Lily screamed. "Shut up and listen to me!"

Karen fell back, covering her mouth. Immediately, Howard Jamison was on his feet. "Are you going to let her talk to her mother that way?"

"You too!" Lily yelled at him. "You listen, too, you big... *you big...*"

He leaned over the table in front of Coburn, his face red. "You're going to tolerate this?"

"Is Lily being so disrespectful?" Coburn asked. "She's following the rules—something she's very good at. I told her to scream if she had to, and she's screaming. It's time, Mr. Jamison, that your daughter found her own voice."

"Please, Howard, sit down," came from Lily's mother.

He sat down, but his jaw was working, and a vein stood out in his temple. Juju left her coloring and climbed onto her father's lap, searching his face with big eyes.

"I'm finished, anyway," Lily said in a voice that was barely audible. She *was* finished. Finished and shaking, her heart thumping in her throat. She'd almost called her father a big baboon!

The room was quiet for a while. At last Coburn spoke. "You did very well expressing yourself, Lily. That wasn't easy. It wasn't easy for your parents to hear, either. Karen and Howard ...I'm proud of you. You've all taken a giant step today."

Juju wriggled down then and ran around the table to stand beside Coburn. "I need to go to the bathroom," she said.

It was a laugh they all needed. Coburn hugged Juju, who had already started hopping. "Hey, you're wonderful, you know that? You won't let us take ourselves too seriously, will you? Come on, let's all take a break. The trays will be here any minute. And over lunch, *you* get to talk." She poked a finger at Juju's chest.

They all stood. Juju went back to her mother, who seemed glad to be leaving the room for whatever reason. Howard Jamison walked to the window, looked out, walked back, cleared his throat.

"Sorry," he said to Dr. Coburn, who was placing the chairs back around the table. "I don't always know what's going on here, I guess."

She gave him a gleaming Coburn smile, her blue eyes warm behind the big glasses.

"You're doing fine," she said. "In some ways, you know, therapy is like playing a game. It takes awhile to learn what the moves mean."

Her father stood there, hands in his pockets. "Games I understand. Winners, losers, I know all about that."

"When family therapy works, everyone wins."

Lily wasn't sure she knew what was going on, either, but suddenly she knew she wasn't the only deficient member of this family. Her mother—her strong, Herculean mother—had crumpled before her eyes. Her father had actually sassed back, had stood up for his wife. And as yet, Coburn hadn't said one word about Lily's eating habits.

[169]

When the trays came, it was Lily's mother who merely picked at her seafood salad and left her luncheon roll on the plate. Lily ate everything she'd ordered, though she let Juju take one or two tastes of her Jell-O.

Her mother frowned at them sternly, her expression saying, "That isn't polite."

Lily might have felt rebuked, but about then Coburn handed her a carrot curl off her own plate. "I know you like these Lily, and they gave me too many."

She held up another one. "Anyone else want a carrot curl?"

Karen looked horrified, but Juju accepted Coburn's offering and ate it with more crunch than Lily thought possible.

Twenty-three

Franklin Rogers slipped down the fifth-floor corridor ahead of the others, motioning them to stay back as he neared room 528. He was breathing hard. He figured there might be some rule about visiting *en masse*, but so far no one had stopped them. He stuck his head in at Lily's open doorway.

There she was, lying across the bed in her jeans—studying, of all things! A book and notebook lay open beside her. She didn't move. She hadn't seen him. He stepped back with the other cheerleaders, mouthing instructions. At Franklin's signal, Cory held a large embellished poster in the doorway with the one word *we* printed on it. All together they began humming the Clarkson pep song through their teeth, sounding exactly like a kazoo band that never found time to practice.

Franklin could see Lily through the doorway as she sat up and started laughing. "Who's out there?" she said.

The "we" poster disappeared and one saying "love" took its place.

"Hey!" She was up on her knees.

Finally, the word "Lily" danced its way into position for her to see, and they ended the pep song in two-part harmony. Just in time, too. An officious-looking nurse was walking down the hall toward them.

Lily came out of the room and was immediately surrounded. Cory grabbed her, passed her along to Eric and Wendy. "You guys!" she kept saying, looking very happy to see them. Franklin had never seen her look so happy, in fact. She was still skinny. After nearly four weeks in the hospital, she should have looked more improved. But she did look lots happier.

The nurse arrived, herself smiling, and motioned them to go on into Lily's room.

"We could use a little more pep on this floor," she said as the cheerleaders crammed themselves into 528, "but there's a ceiling on noise."

"Kids," Lily said, "this is Peggy McPherson, who gets on my case all the time."

"Secretly, she loves me," McPherson winked. "Keep the door closed, Lily."

Suddenly they were all talking at once. Lily could tell they were nervous, especially the sophomores, who mostly stood. Franklin had helped himself to one of the chairs, and the varsity kids piled on the bed with Lily. Everyone exclaimed at how much better she looked and how much they'd missed her and how lucky she was to get a vacation from school.

"I'm getting out Sunday," she told them. "I should be back in school next week. I'm so sick of this place I could *die*!"

"A present," Jean Callaghan said as she edged up to the bed and handed Lily a cake box. "Franklin made it himself."

"Oh, no!" someone said. There were gagging sounds.

Slitting the Scotch tape with a long fingernail, Lily carefully opened the box and peeked in. A chocolate layer cake with deep, swirling frosting looked back at her. One piece was missing.

"Rogers!" she exclaimed. "Did you sample this?"

Everyone roared.

"I couldn't help myself. I knew you'd understand." He ducked as Lily's pillow came flying across the room. "It was a joke, honest!"

The others crowded close to see the cake with the missing wedge.

"You can eat it now if you want to," Franklin said, looking at it with more than proprietary interest.

Lily grinned. "Okay, let's cut it. We'll have a party!" She looked around. "My kingdom for a knife..."

"I brought one." Franklin was on his feet, reaching into his back pocket. The cheerleaders hooted at him again. "You really take the cake!" Cory punned. Suddenly Lily realized how much she'd missed being with them.

After she dispatched Wendy to the bathroom for paper towels, the party was under way, with Franklin brandishing his plastic cutlery like a Benihana chef.

Lily was given the first, and biggest, piece. A month ago, the idea of eating cake would have set off all her panic bells. Even now, she knew she couldn't finish such a big serving, but she'd eat some of it. The best part was that it looked good to her. It hadn't been easy, reconditioning her thinking, moving from $cake = calories + guilt + loss \ of \ control$ to $cake = pleasant \ taste + energy$.

"We'd have been up here sooner," Carol was saying, "but Snell told us not to come."

"Why did she say that?" Lily asked.

"She told us you couldn't have visitors."

Franklin interrupted his cake-cutting. "Yeah, then I saw Eda Mae on the bus and she said she'd been up to see you twice. So we just came ahead."

"Snell sent me this spider plant," Lily said thoughtfully, wondering again how Calypso was faring, "and Eda Mae's been bringing assignments up for me."

"Ms. Snell said you were on the psychiatric floor," Carol said, "and you're not. She's the one who's nuts. She can't get anything straight."

Her choice of words silenced the room for a moment.

"She probably misunderstood," Lily said, wiping frosting off her fingers. "I really couldn't have visitors at first. This cake looks delicious, Franklin. I'll bet your mother made it."

"You kidding?" He handed the last sliver to Carol. "Say... I brought you something else." He squeezed his hand into his pants pocket and finally extracted a saucer-size lapel pin.

"I'm running for student senate this spring." He beamed at Lily. "Wanted you to have my first campaign button." He boldly pinned it in the middle of her sweat shirt, causing Lily to suck in to protect herself. "Collect originals!" it said, with Franklin's round face laughing out from below the words. There were cheers and whistles when Lily impulsively reached out and hooked her arm around his neck.

"Congratulations!" she said. "I know you'll make it."

"Yeah..." He was blushing. "I probably will. Everybody loves a fat man."

"Who can cook," Lily added, taking another small bite of cake.

Franklin stayed on after the others left, explaining that his mother was picking him up on her way home from work.

"Can't you drive yet?" Lily needled him.

He ignored her, pretending to be studying Juju's drawings that decorated the walls. He posed in front of each one, stroking his chin, making like some big art connoisseur.

"Hmm, excellent primitives. Who's the artist?"

"My little sister, of course."

Coburn had given Lily Juju's drawings from the last two family sessions to add to her collection. Hers was now the most color-ful room on the floor. Visitors came daily to view her gallery, and the little contribution box she'd set up—"Support the Arts" —already had eighty-six cents in it. She was planning to throw a party for the nurses when she left.

"Is this one the family portrait?" Franklin asked.

Lily nodded. "Look how big my mother is in that picture! That's supposed to mean something."

"Yeah, but you're almost as big as she is."

"No, that's Juju," Lily explained, jumping to her feet. "You can see what an exaggerated ego she has. I'm the horizontal one in a hospital bed. There."

"Shows what I know. I thought that was part of the scenery."

Lily smiled ruefully. She had been part of the scenery that day.

Franklin glanced at his watch, then returned to sprawl in the armchair once again.

Lily sat cross-legged on the bed, studying her campaign button.

"Franklin, I know it was your idea to bring everybody up here. I really appreciate it. I was starting to talk to myself. Honest, this place gets morbid."

"Haven't you seen...what's her name?...who lives by you?"

"Erica? Yeah, she's been here, but all she talks about is her boyfriends. Room 528 hasn't exactly been Circus Circus."

"You know what?" Franklin said, crossing his arms. "I was thinking of asking you to manage my campaign this spring."

"Oh, good grief!"

"But Snell told me not to ask you until you were back in school and feeling better, so I won't."

"You're all heart, you and Snell."

Franklin grinned. "Well, think about it, anyway. We could pull it off, you and I. You know, we have more in common than our food obsessions."

"*I'm* not obsessed with food!"

"Well, whatever you call it. I'm obsessed, I admit it. Look at me!" He punched his big belly.

"But I like being thin," Lily said. "I'm never going to get over a hundred and ten. If I do, I'll go back on a diet."

"Where do you get the willpower?"

She shrugged. "That's what I have most of. You know, you should talk to my psychiatrist. She's really helped me understand a lot about myself. Weight disorders are her specialty."

"Yeah, but I was born fat. You ought to see my mother."

"You ought to see mine," Lily said. "I never thought she'd ever be eating desserts. Dr. Coburn says she has anorexic tendencies of her own. Now she's gaining weight, too. But I never want to be a hundred and twenty-nine again. I was huge!"

"Tell me about it!" Franklin snorted. "Look, I'm shorter than you and weigh twice as much. I'm the one with problems. No girl's ever going out with me."

Lily agreed. Then she thought of the fat girl she'd often seen in Dr. Coburn's waiting room and knew that someone, somewhere...

"Hey, really, why don't you get an appointment with Dr. Coburn? She's super. And going to a shrink isn't what you think at all."

He raised his eyebrows. "Do you lie on a couch?"

"Where have *you* been? Coburn doesn't even have a couch. She goes running with me. Can you believe that? My dad thinks she's pretty unorthodox, but that's what I like about her."

"Aw, I don't know." Franklin looked down at his pudgy hands. "I'm probably one of those people who live to eat." He pursed his lips. Lily could tell he was already thinking about dinner.

"Boy, do you give up easy!" she said, scooting to the edge of the bed.

Franklin stood and walked to the window, searching the circle below for his mother's car. "That's easy for you to say, Lily. You've never been fat—never! Look at the dainty way you picked at your cake...you don't care about food like I do."

"Look, Franklin, I've been signing these contracts with Dr. Coburn. If I gain so much, I get some special privilege. That's the way it works here in the hospital. Why don't the two of us draw up a contract and do the same thing? You take off the pounds I put on."

Franklin looked skeptical, standing there studying Lily's face from behind his gold-frame glasses. "What's the reward?" he asked at last.

"I'll get you elected to the student senate."

Franklin didn't bat an eye. "Will you go out with me...once? To a movie? And manage my campaign besides?"

Lily saw that his ears had turned a fiery red. He *was* fat. Even his ears were fat, but she couldn't turn him down.

"Okay," she agreed, "but you drive a hard bargain."

Later, Lily stood at her window watching Franklin get into his car five stories below. He looked up at the last minute, but she was sure he didn't see her wave. "Crazy Franklin," she said under her breath. He'd spent his last ten minutes with her talking about famous historical figures whose lives were guided by older women. She'd nearly croaked when he referred to her as an "older woman," deciding then and there that their first date would also be their last.

Lily turned back around to regard the dinner tray which had just arrived. She sighed. If only eating weren't so necessary! She had begun to understand why she had starved herself, was actually accepting the fact that her anorexia was a plea for attention and independence, but *knowing* and *doing* were still two different things. She rolled the tray to one side and stretched out on her bed.

"*I* think you quit eating because you didn't want to grow up."

It was Erica's voice from a week ago, saying words that Lily couldn't get out of her head once she'd heard them.

"What makes you say that?" Lily had asked her.

"I read about anorexia in a magazine. The girl in the article fits you to a *t*."

Erica could say things like that. She'd conduct an analysis right in front of you, whether she knew what she was talking about or not.

"That's ridiculous," Lily was quick to defend herself, "everybody has to grow up. I know that."

"But everybody doesn't *want* to."

"Erica, you're... that's nonsense."

"No, listen. Every time I talk about John or having a relationship... or... or anything like that... you cringe. Like sex is dirty or something. I think you're afraid of maturing, like this other girl who had anorexia."

At that point, Erica had plopped down on the bed and given Lily this really direct look. "Have you ever kissed a guy? Be honest with me, now, I'm always honest with you. Have you ever?"

Lily thought of Cory pressing his hot mouth against hers at cheerleader camp, pinning her arms so she couldn't resist. "Of course I've kissed someone!"

"Did you like it?"

"No, I hated it."

"See?" Erica tossed her dark hair over her shoulder with an impatient gesture. "That's what I mean. You had a bad experience and it scared you. But it's not that way when you meet someone you really like. Being in love is..."

Lily sat up. She didn't want an instant replay of Erica's rhapsody on love. That would really spoil her dinner! But she couldn't erase the picture of Erica's face when she told her about Mark Davis, the new guy she'd met at John's fraternity.

"This is it, Lily!" She was glowing as she said it. "He's the one, I can tell."

Erica and she were so different.

But Erica hadn't stopped there. She was still pushing Lily to confide. "Isn't there anyone you like?"

"I like a lot of people."

Erica grinned. "Did you know I had a crush on Daniel once? I did. The summer I was thirteen. I flirted with him like crazy, but he was more interested in Pillow Ticking than in me. I nearly died because he wouldn't pay attention to me."

"You never told me that."

"Oh, well," Erica said quietly, "everybody loves Daniel. You do, don't you?"

Somehow, Lily had managed to end that conversation, but she'd thought about it every single day since it had taken place.

The hard truth was that she didn't feel comfortable with most of the guys she knew. Only with the ones who didn't threaten her in some way. See how quickly she'd promised Franklin Rogers a date! He was "safe." So was Daniel. And she did love him, Erica was right. She always would. And she trusted him...implicitly.

Maybe she was afraid of sex and growing up. Maybe Erica had hit on something. Her own mother's message, both spoken and unspoken, was that sex should be deferred—perhaps forever! As in everything else, Lily supposed, she'd picked up all her clues from Karen Jamison.

Coburn was seeing the family again tomorrow. Lily would bring it up. "Let's talk about sex today," she'd say right off and watch her parents disintegrate.

Lily took the lid off her dinner and inhaled. Broccoli in cheese sauce with baked halibut. Her favorites. For once they'd gotten her order straight and left out the potatoes. Maybe she'd eat everything tonight.

Twenty-four

Lily stepped out of the wheelchair and right into Peggy McPherson's arms. It didn't matter that it was snowing or that the door of the Buick stood open or that McPherson was shivering without a coat. They gave each other a long embrace, squishing Lily's pillow in the process.

"You'd better come back and see us," McPherson said. "But not as a patient, of course!"

"I will, I promise. And tell Pritchart the purple finger painting is hers. She deserves it."

They laughed at Lily's joke.

Then Lily got into the back beside Juju, waving at her nurse as Howard Jamison pulled the car away from the curb. Lily found herself totally unprepared for the sharp sense of loss she was experiencing.

She'd been so eager to get out of the hospital, and now she really was going home. Wasn't this what she'd been waiting for? Her mother was chattering away in the front seat; Juju was leaning against her in the back, giving her big, shy grins. Lily hugged Juju on one side and her patchwork pillow on the other and realized she was scared. This was the day she'd dreamed about, and she was *scared*.

Could it happen to her again? Could the anorexia start all over? Their therapy would go on for six months or a year, but Coburn said they were beginning to interact like a healthy family already. Even her father was warming to Coburn's personality. What did Lily have to be afraid about?

"A big envelope from Radcliffe arrived yesterday." Her mother turned around to look at her. "Hope you don't mind my opening it. The pictures made me positively homesick."

Lily minded, all right, but she didn't make a fuss about it.

"I may not be going to Radcliffe," she said. "I may stay here and go to the U., I haven't decided." She saw her father reach over and touch her mother. Some message passed between them.

"It's your decision, of course," her mother said.

Lily returned to looking out the window. Everything was scary. Especially being in charge of her own life.

Lily's heart began to beat faster as her father left the boulevard and turned down Danish Road, where the landmarks greeted her like old friends. They drove past the sugar mill, stolid and gray, its two stories of empty windows haunted with yesterday's ghosts. Exactly a mile farther, they'd come to the old abandoned church.

As they neared the snow-shrouded structure, Lily's eye caught on a figure standing there at the opposite side of the road. An old lady, shaking an umbrella, was trying to attract a passing car, which swerved but didn't stop.

Suddenly Lily cried out, "That's Grandma Perry! What's she doing?"

"Howard, slow down," her mother said.

Her dad slowed, then braked. "I'd swear she's trying to hitch a ride."

He rolled down his window and called to her, but Grandma Perry didn't recognize them or their car. "Wrong way, wrong way!" she called out, motioning them to go on.

Finally, Lily's dad got out and crossed to where she stood. Hearing Juju giggling behind her hands, Lily had a hard time keeping her own face straight. At last, Grandma Perry accepted Howard Jamison's arm, looking more and more pleased as they neared the car.

"I was on my way to see Lily," she said, closing the umbrella, then ducking into the back seat, "and here she is, right here." An ice-cold hand gripped Lily's. "This is about the best piece of luck I ever had."

"Were you really on your way to see me?"

Karen turned around. "I'm so glad we came by just when we did."

At the same time, Lily's father asked, "Where to now, Mrs. Perry?"

"Straight home," she said, chortling. "Wait till I tell Daniel about this. I'd been plannin' all week to pay you a visit, Lily. Guess I waited that much too long. But it all comes out all right, don't it?"

Lily patted the pillow Grandma Perry had made for her. "I wish you'd heard the nurses' nice compliments on your feather stitch. Dr. Coburn said she'd give anything for a pillow like this."

"You took that old thing with you?" Grandma Perry sounded pleased in spite of her scolding. "It wasn't even sanitary, was it?"

Lily and her dad exchanged smiles in the rearview mirror.

"I love it," Lily said. "It's one of my favorite things."

Pulling into the driveway at the top of Oak Grove, Lily offered to see Grandma Perry into her house. When Lily was invited to stay and have a cup of tea, she was surprised at how eagerly she accepted, how glad she was to postpone her own homecoming.

"We'll have our visit right here," the little grandmother said, bustling out of her coat and into an apron. "The folks is all gone today. Lucky me! We'll just have us a nice tea party all by ourselves."

Lily sat at the kitchen table, feeling the raised roses on the teacup while Daniel's grandmother put on a kettle. The room was warm and cozy. As always, Lily felt enormously comfortable here.

"I see you're eatin' again," Grandma Perry said. "Got a little meat on your bones."

"I'm about ninety-eight pounds."

"My, my. Still have a ways to go, but you're lookin' better than you did. It takes time, don't it?"

Lily nodded.

"Same as me when I was a youngster. Couldn't eat. Didn't care a thing for eatin'. My mama said I was born puny, looked like a pink-skinned rat." She chuckled as she poured boiling water into a teapot.

"Mama was so low they had to get me a wet nurse. She called me 'Little Mulie'...'cause I was so stubborn, I guess. And, you know, that name stuck for years. Once they give you a nickname in the South, that's what they call you."

"What *is* your first name?" Lily asked.

"I have three of 'em—Victoria Elizabeth Anne!" She beamed across the table at Lily. "Mama always thought queens was so grand."

"What beautiful names," Lily said, thinking that "Little Mulie" fit her better. No wonder Daniel had so much self-esteem, coming from a grandma as positive and persistent as this one.

"When it came to namin' my own babies, though, I went straight to the Bible. Didn't want my children called by no animal names!"

"*Daniel* comes from the Bible, doesn't it?" Lily mused.

"Oh, my, yes. Daniel in the lion's den, remember that story?"

What Lily was remembering right then was Daniel's face when he told her about his tribulations at the U. He was in a lion's den, all right.

She watched as Grandma Perry poured the tea into china cups.

"I saw a show on TV once," Lily said, "where this man claimed that people grow to fit their names...that we fulfill our predictions or something. I wonder if it's true."

Grandma Perry sat up straight as a pin. "I believe there's something to that. My son Paul became a teacher!"

Lily sipped at her tea, smiling and wondering. "Let's see, now, how could anyone live up to my name? Really. Lilies are so beautiful and so...so perfect...."

"You're already like your name," Grandma Perry said, her eyes shining. "That was a smart man on TV. A lovely white flower, that's exactly what you are."

Lily's cheeks grew warm. "And *you* make lovely tea!" she said, her laugh and Grandma Perry's bubbling up together.

It was after seven that night when Lily finally saw Daniel again. She had spent the afternoon studying, had gotten through her first meal with the family, had tried on a whole rack of school clothes to find something to wear the next day. At last, when she couldn't stand it any longer, she decided she would call Daniel. Contrary to all the etiquette she'd been taught, *she* would call *him*.

"All you have to do is assert yourself," Coburn had told her more than once.

"Well, that's exactly what I'm doing," Lily said under her breath as she picked up the receiver and dialed.

Ten minutes later, Lily was waiting in the gazebo for Daniel. It had started snowing again, big, lazy flakes, but it wasn't very cold. Nonetheless, she'd bundled up in a heavy coat and brought two blankets for them to sit on.

"Juju is not invited," she'd told her mother on her way out of the house. "Daniel and I haven't talked for a long time."

Her mother had given her an uncertain look before answering. "I'll keep her in."

Lily actually smiled at her mother when she told her, "Thanks."
She hadn't done that in a long time.

In the gazebo, Lily took off her gloves to light the candle inside the glass cylinder. There was sputtering and flickering, then a steady flame. She centered the candle on the round table. With cold fingers she worked the twistee off the bag of marshmallows. She and Daniel had toasted marshmallows in the winter once before, but it had been ages ago.

Now the screen door of the gazebo rattled.

"This the Dead Goat Saloon?" came a deep voice.

"You got it!" Lily said and laughed.

Daniel ducked as he entered the gazebo, then straightened and put out a hand. They shook hands, of all things! "Like it's been a long journey," he said, stamping the snow off his boots.

"Same here, old-timer. Sit down and warm your hands at the fire."

Daniel scooted in on the circular bench. He rubbed his hands together over the flame as he'd been told.

"Remember when—" they said at the same time, then burst out laughing.

"Only it was at your place," Lily reminded him.

"In the hideout—"

"In a worse snowstorm than this."

Daniel pushed back his wool cap. "What had we been reading then?"

"*To Build a Fire*," Lily said. "Wasn't that it?"

"Yeah! There we were, right down to our last match, winds howling, temperature eighty below or something, and you come up with a bag of marshmallows."

Gleefully, Lily pulled two forks from her coat pocket. "Ta-da! We didn't have any utensils before. You had to crawl around on the creekbed after some sticks. Remember?"

Daniel rested his arms on the table, smiling. He looked at Lily.

"Considering our common history, you sure have avoided me this year."

Lily looked down, feeling as if she'd just been stabbed.

"I was going to visit you again, try to win some of my money back, but I didn't think you wanted me to. You said you'd call, remember?"

"I know. I haven't exactly been myself through all this."

"Are you better now?"

"I hope!"

"You look lots better, all cured and everything."

"Cured, no. I guess anorexia might be something like alcoholism, in that a person has to go on dealing with it. But"—she raised a gloved finger—"Dr. Coburn says the prognosis is very good now that the whole family's in treatment."

"Man, that's great. I guess you're a reformed anorectic, then. You know, you scared me in the hospital, you were so skinny."

"I still have a way to go, as your grandmother reminded me."

Daniel chuckled. "She doesn't mince words, does she? Did she tell you about me?"

"No. What do you mean?"

"I've had some counseling myself the past couple of weeks."

"But you're still in school—"

"Guess again." He tilted the candle and watched the wax run.

"Daniel, what'd you do?"

"I decided I had to be in the wrong field. I went to the U. career counseling center, took a whole battery of tests. They all said the same thing: Math and science were my lowest scores."

"But what will you do now?" Lily asked "What about your future?"

"I'll work a couple of quarters. In the fall I think I'll get into the college of education, where I belong. I've always wanted to be an elementary-school teacher." He admitted it grudgingly. "Big, *macho* job, huh?"

"Daniel, I love it! You'd make a marvelous teacher. Like fa-ther, like son."

"Dad can have them at the other end. I'd rather start them out."

Daniel reached into the plastic bag Lily handed him and worked a marshmallow onto the tines of his fork.

"Can you find a job?" she asked as she moved the candle closer to Daniel. "Here, you toast the first one."

"No, go ahead." He shoved it back. "Ladies first."

"Not anymore." She moved it again "Be my guest."

They started laughing.

"I'm bigger," he said, making broad shoulders.

"It's my gazebo!" She stuck out her chin.

They jammed their marshmallows together over the flame, laughing like goons. Finally, in the interest of conversation, Lily withdrew hers.

"I already have a job," Daniel said. "Heard about the opening through my mom. I'll be driving the Head Start bus beginning next month, doing playground and kitchen duty betweentimes. It'll give me a taste of what it's like dealing with the little monsters."

"Daniel, that's wonderful! The kids are going to love you."

"Well, I don't know about that..."

Daniel handed his toasted marshmallow to Lily, at the same time taking her fork out of her hand. "You always burn yours," he said, covering up his gallantry.

She made a face at him but accepted the bubbly marshmallow, which was already beginning to droop. "One's enough for me," she said. "The rest are yours."

"You know something, Lily?" Daniel stared at the flame. "I was afraid you'd gotten ...color-conscious."

Lily pulled back. "Me? I thought *you* had. When I saw you with Kimberly that night."

Daniel laughed. He leaned back and stretched out his legs, trying to engineer two marshmallows onto one fork but finally giving up.

"You know what? I really think we should back up and start over. Let's say it's September, okay?"

Lily nodded. She'd give anything to start the school year over.

"I've just arrived home from Stanford. I've watched you run and can tell you need a hell of a lot of coaching."

Lily smiled, knowing what was coming. "And I suppose an old track man like you finds himself just itching to teach me a thing or two."

"Right! So I take you in hand and we begin to train together, build up your stamina and monitor that heart rate."

Suddenly Daniel sat forward. His eyes had little points of light in them. "Hey, you know what I want to do? I'd like to qualify for that *Tribune* marathon next summer. I'll have more time to run now. What do you think? You want to go for it?"

"I'd love to," Lily said, knowing she'd be lucky to log five miles.

A random snowflake made its way into the gazebo and sizzled in the flame.

"Of course, you'd have to eat right, get your strength back"— he hesitated—"and you'd probably want to invite me to the Sports Mall while the weather's bad. You know, so we could run inside for a while."

"Consider yourself invited."

Daniel grinned sheepishly. "Was that sneaky enough? The way I wormed that invitation out of you?"

"Pretty sneaky."

"Well, you know what they say—it takes a sneak to know a sneak!"

Daniel threw back his head to roar at his own joke, unmindful of the sneak who had just stolen his perfectly toasted marshmallow and was popping it into her own mouth.